Deceived
by a Duke

An All's Fair in Love Novella

By Erin Knightley

Deceived by a Duke

Copyright © 2014 by Erin Knightley

ISBN: 1500668664
ISBN-13: 978-1500668662

Dedication

To my parents, for inspiring Libby's multilingual response to Philip's very important question. And because your 44 years of marriage (and counting!) is very inspiring, indeed!

And for Kirk, even though it's a pretty good bet that, after all these years, you're not really a duke masquerading as a gentleman. Although, if you are, I'd totally be cool with it!

Books By Erin Knightley:

The SEALED WITH A KISS Series
More Than a Stranger
A Taste for Scandal
Flirting with Fortune
Miss Mistletoe – A Penguin eSpecial

The PRELUDE TO A KISS Series
The Baron Next Door
The Earl I Adore (January 2015)
The Duke Can Go to the Devil (Fall 2015)

The ALL'S FAIR IN LOVE Series (Novellas)
Ruined by a Rake
Scandalized by a Scoundrel
Deceived by a Duke

Chapter One

"*E*xplain to me again why staying in this hovel and being called 'mister' by those well below the both of us is a good idea?"

Philip Dain, Duke of Gillingham, sent a withering look to his brother, who was draped across the room's only sofa like Caesar awaiting peeled grapes and palm fronds. Philip possessed the obligatory fraternal love for Nigel, and he even liked the man from time to time, but after five days of travel over both land and sea, his brother was riding Philip's last nerve.

Sweeping his hand to encompass the classic furnishings, freshly papered walls, and crystal-and-gold sconces, Philip said, "I believe your definition of *hovel* needs some adjustment. This is one of the finest inns in the city, if not all of Spain."

"Which is precisely why we should have rented a townhouse, like any normal civilized gentleman."

Philip lifted an imperious eyebrow. "Remarkably, I am both a civilized gentleman *and* satisfied with our accommodations. As for the second part of your question, you know full well that I wanted a true holiday for once in my life, without people scrutinizing my every move or bowing and scraping and 'Your Gracing' me every time I turn around."

Nigel snorted, propping one booted foot up on the immaculate oval table before him. "Yes, yes. Poor Duke, so tired of always getting everything his heart desires."

If ever Philip had entertained any doubts about the plan he and his mother had concocted in regards to Nigel, they would have been obliterated in that one moment. Only a spoiled, self-entitled eighteen-year-old pup could conjure that sort of insolence. It was galling—especially since they had no one to blame but themselves.

Stalking to the sofa, Philip slapped his brother's feet from the furniture. "Whether referred to as duke, lord, or mister, one must always show respect for others, *including* for their property."

His brother glared up at him but didn't defy him. Instead, he stretched out and put his hands behind his head. "As you say, *Mr.* Westbrook."

It was the name Philip had settled on before they departed England. It made the most sense to use one of his lesser titles: Viscount Westbrook. His other titles—Marquis of Cuxton and Duke of Gillingham—were far too recognizable to use.

"I do say," he retorted, "and so will you if you expect a penny before your next birthday." He paused to suck in a deep, temper-cooling breath. He was not here to be baited into arguments.

Nigel's laugh was short and hollow. "Have no fear, big brother. You know you've got me by the bollocks. Not a word of your station until we touch English soil again."

Not the expression Philip would have used, but it was accurate enough. "It was your choice to bet money you didn't have on a game you knew nothing about. You should be grateful I'm offering even the *possibility* of additional funds. I can assure you, it is the last time I will bail you out of a situation like this."

Settling on the closest chair, a neutrally upholstered wingback positioned perpendicular to the couch, Philip blew out a long breath. They had only just arrived, and he didn't want to start off on the wrong foot. "Seville is supposed to be one of the finest cities on the continent, and it's rebounded well in the years since the war. I'd simply like to enjoy it in anonymity so that we can be free to truly relax."

Nigel sent a sideways glance Philip's way, his dark-blue eyes glinting with renewed mischief. "Anonymity? Ah, I see. You wish to be able to sin in peace."

Philip gritted his teeth. He wanted to tell his brother to shut his damn mouth, but he wasn't going to justify Nigel's purposeful crudeness with a response. Yes, it was the way of young peacocks these days, to strut like pigeons and banter like sailors, but that was precisely why they were here. Philip and their mother had spent so much time compensating for the trauma of the old duke's death, which played out not five feet from Nigel's horrified young eyes, that they hadn't taken a firm enough hand in raising him these last three years.

It was a mistake he planned to right on this trip. First, he'd stripped them of the special treatment they would have received had the inn known Philip's status as a duke. Next, he would spend the whole of their time here—four long weeks—being the role model he should have been all along, demonstrating the proper way to respect others. And if this little intervention somehow failed, Philip wasn't opposed to ditching Nigel on the Channel Islands on the way home.

"Well," he said, slapping his hands against the tops of his thighs, "I believe I'll stretch my legs a bit after being cooped up for so long. Care to join me for a walk through the city?"

Nigel scoffed and tugged at the open collar of his shirt. His cravat was draped over the arm of the sofa, while his jacket had never made it past the table in the small entryway. "I'd sooner walk bare-arsed through the pub than get dressed again—particularly since you didn't see fit to bring your man along."

Patience, patience. The next four weeks were going to be the longest of Philip's life. Nodding tersely, he said, "Suit yourself. I'll be back within the hour, at which time we can discuss dinner." He strode to the entryway and shrugged into his jacket. Already he was itching for the freedom Seville's streets offered, where no one would recognize him. That hadn't been the purpose of their trip, but it was a side effect of which he planned to take full advantage.

"Wait."

Philip paused in the process of retrieving his hat and raised an eyebrow.

His brother pushed off the couch and stretched,

4

his long arms nearly touching the dark wooden beam above him. "On second thought, we're stuck at an inn with no entertainment, no decent liquor, and no females to speak of. I might as well join you. Hopefully we can find a place to purchase some respectable spirits, at least."

Philip shouldn't have been surprised. Nigel had been rather vocal about his disappointment when he'd discovered the inn served only ale, sangria, wine, and sherry. He waited while Nigel put himself to rights—unhurriedly—before leading the way to the street below.

The warm, damp air that greeted him as he opened the front door was exactly what he needed. It didn't matter that he had stepped off the boat not two hours ago; the sea air was always the one thing that could calm him, no matter how frayed his nerves. Of course, the water from the Seville harbor was brackish at best this far from the ocean, but it would do.

Turning right, he set off toward the waterfront, trusting that Nigel would keep pace. The narrow street wended between close-set buildings, blocking out any sunlight that might have otherwise heated the cobblestone pavers. It would have felt like home had it not been for the foreign words spoken by those around them. The Spanish language had never been his strong suit, though his years of French lessons helped bridge the gap of understanding, if only a little.

He would have preferred to go someplace like Belgium for this trip, but the likelihood of encountering someone there who knew him as a duke was much too high for his liking. It made more sense to travel to Spain, which was close enough to make the journey worthwhile

while parliament was adjourned but far enough from the more commonly traveled routes that they'd likely go unnoticed.

He kept his eyes on the road ahead as he walked, avoiding eye contact with passersby. It was a tactic he had discovered three years ago, when he'd first taken up the title and learned how often people wished to catch the eye of a duke. It was one thing for which his height was exceptionally useful.

"This city isn't quite as dreadful as first feared," Nigel said, his face tipped back as he took in the towering three- and four-story buildings around them. "Perhaps there is civilization here after all."

Philip gave a little snort. "You were expecting caves and stone huts, perhaps? Seville is considered to be the cultural heart of Spain."

"My, what a distinction," his brother said, sarcasm dripping from the words like melted wax.

"I assure you, brother—England isn't the only country in the world with a rich heritage of artists, musicians, and philosophers."

A sharp jerk at Philip's sleeve brought him up short. He turned to find a thin, dark-haired street merchant with a scarred cheek and missing front tooth. The man utter a few terse words, then gestured back toward a vegetable cart Philip had just passed. Apparently the vendors here weren't afraid to be aggressive. Pulling his sleeve from the man's grasp, Philip held up a hand and said sternly, "No, thank you."

Not taking the hint, the merchant shook his head and spoke again, this time more fervently. If this was how all the city's vendors were, this was not going to be a pleasant trip.

"Let me guess," Nigel said, his hands at his hips as he observed the exchange. "One of Socrates's contemporaries?"

Philip spared a scowl for his brother before turning back to the man. His brow pinched in displeasure. *"No hablo español."* It was exactly one third of his Spanish vocabulary, along with "My name is" and "A pint of ale, please."

Instead of backing away, the man began to speak slower, exaggerating each syllable as though it would magically overcome the language barrier. He moved his hands in worthless gestures that didn't help in the least. People were beginning to stare—something Philip hated. He started to turn, wanting nothing so much as to leave the earnestly speaking man and the gathered gawkers behind.

"Wait!"

The single English word, spoken in a high, clear feminine voice, instantly captured his attention.

He glanced in the direction from which the voice had originated and saw her at once: a blond-haired, fair-skinned young woman who stood out among the crowd. Her white-and-blue gown was of superior quality, as was the fashionable bonnet perched at a jaunty angle atop her golden curls. She possessed the sort of features poets and dreamers loved to go on about, but Philip settled on one word: lovely.

"Yes?" he said, quite at a loss of how else to respond. He sensed more than saw his brother's piqued interest as the younger man sidled closer to him.

The woman stepped forward, her wide-set,

7

cognac-colored eyes meeting his without the least amount of hesitation. Everything about her shouted well-born miss, yet she clearly had no compunction about speaking to a man to whom she had not yet been introduced. "He's trying to tell you that you dropped some coins beneath his booth. He would have brought them to you, but he didn't wish to lose you in the crowd."

Philip glanced back at the man, who now looked slightly annoyed. He'd been trying to act honorably, and Philip had written him off. Turning back to the girl, he said, "Am I to assume you speak the language?"

She grinned, revealing a perfect row of white, slightly rounded teeth. "I do, though not half as well as I speak French and Italian. Or Latin, for that matter. It's terribly ironic that the first time I should leave England, it should be for Spain instead of France or Italy."

"Libby," her companion said, her voice vaguely chiding. "We really should be on our way." The other woman was tall and somewhat older, perhaps in her mid-twenties, with neat dark hair and pretty blue eyes that seemed to size him up in a glance. She didn't look terribly impressed.

"Please," he said, interrupting the woman's attempts to hurry Libby away. "I simply wish for my apologies to be conveyed to the poor man. If you would, please tell him he may keep the coins as my thanks."

With a small nod, she glanced to the merchant and spoke, her words a jumble of tongue-rolling Spanish. Until that very moment, Philip had never considered the Spanish language to be particularly appealing. Clearly he'd been wrong.

The vendor raised his bushy brows at their translator, then offered Philip a wide grin and a sound slap on the shoulder. More foreign words poured forth before he hurried back to his cart. A young boy manned the leafy green vegetables, his arms akimbo with his knobby elbows poking through the holes in his sleeves. The vendor gave him a fierce hug before directing the child to retrieve the money.

Nigel shifted, his blue gaze settling squarely on the girl, Libby. "You were holding out on us," he said with what Philip could only imagine was his brother's attempt at a rakish grin. "That was quite a bit more than merely passable Spanish."

Philip was oddly disappointed in the girl when she blushed and bit back a pleased grin, blossoming like a morning glory in the first rays of dawn. "Thank you, sir, but truly it is not my best. To the unschooled ear it's fine, but I assure you every native Spanish speaker cringes when I open my mouth."

"Not possible," Nigel replied with an authoritative shake of his head. "Not with lips as lovely as yours."

Oh, for Christ's sake. Philip stepped forward quickly, purposely jabbing his brother in the back with his elbow as he nodded politely to the woman. "Please allow me to extend my most fervent thanks for you help. Both your time and your talents are appreciated."

Her mouth relaxed into an easy smile as she shifted her attention to him. "Think nothing of it. I'm thrilled to have my so-called talent be of use. I must say, that was terribly kind of you," she continued, glancing back to the vendor. "He offered you blessings and

9

sincere thanks in return."

Her grin seemed to light her entire countenance, and he was surprised to find himself taking a step toward her. "As I seem to have found myself in a city where I don't speak the language, I'll take all the blessings I can get."

Her eyes widened in mock horror. "You brave souls! I doubt I could bring myself to step foot in a place where I couldn't understand what was going on around me. Of course, that may very well just be the busybody in me speaking."

There was something irrepressible about her that had him smiling back at a near complete stranger as though he regularly consorted with females to whom he'd not been introduced. Or rather, who hadn't been introduced to *him*. As duke, he hadn't had to request an introduction in years.

"Libby," her companion murmured again, her fingers visibly tightening on the girl's arm. "Gabriel will be expecting us shortly."

"Yes, of course," Libby replied mildly, then turned her dark-amber eyes back to the two men. "Best of luck, my fellow countrymen. Just remember, when in doubt, smile and nod. You may agree to a whole manner of things you hadn't intended, but at least you'll be well liked in the process." With a wink, she turned and started away.

"Excellent advice," Nigel called, earning a grin over her shoulder before she disappeared through the low doorway of a nearby shop.

Neither Philip nor his brother moved for a moment, both staring through the cloudy glass to the two figures moving within. It was a singular exchange, just as Libby was a very unique woman. Clearing his throat, Philip slid his gaze to Nigel. "In the future, do please refrain from mentioning a woman's lips before you even know her name."

One corner of Nigel's mouth curled up as he tilted his head. "Whatever for?" he replied, completely without concern. "Women like rakes, and rakes speak out of turn. Not to mention the fact that her lips were well worth the mention."

They had been. A generous bottom lip that pouted without even trying, and a gracefully bowed top that echoed the slender curves of the rest of her. Philip, however, was not about to validate his brother's response. He hadn't realized the man was actually aspiring to be a scoundrel. "You're not a rakehell, for God's sake. We are gentlemen, held to a higher standard, and we should speak accordingly."

Nigel rolled his eyes with such exaggeration, it was a wonder he didn't hurt himself. "God's teeth, but you're a prude. Lighten up, Philip. Every moment in life isn't meant to be so bloody serious."

Prude? "There is a difference between prudishness and respect."

There was also irony in the fact that Philip's rebuttal sounded excessively stuffy, even to his own ears. Still, the accusation chafed like freshly cut hairs caught beneath his collar. He wasn't a rogue, but he sure as hell wasn't a prig, either. Sighing, he swept his hand in the direction they had been headed. "Come on, let's be off to the waterfront. I think the air will do us both some good."

Nigel's teeth flashed as he tossed a mischievous grin toward Philip. "Do you know," he said, cutting his gaze back to the shop window, "I believe I have a better idea."

***

Elizabeth Abbington—Libby to anyone who knew her—grinned broadly as she tugged off her gloves and trailed her fingers over one brightly colored bolt of fabric after another. "And here I thought Spain would have little to offer in the way of entertainment."

Amelia snorted softly and shook her head. "First of all, you thought no such thing, and secondly, I'd hardly call a minor exchange in the middle of the street entertainment. Speaking of which," she said, raising a reproving eyebrow, "you should know by now that one shouldn't speak to strange men on the street."

The mild reprimand was an echo of Amelia's former life, before her husband had pried her from her shell. Back then, every stranger was suspect.

"Strange, no. Gorgeous, yes," Libby replied teasingly, earning the expected eye roll from her friend. "Come now, Amelia. We haven't all been blinded by love. If you could see past that handsome husband of yours, you'd have noticed what fine specimens those gentlemen were."

"*Specimens*? Oh, Libby." Amelia half laughed, half groaned. "What on earth did they teach you at that fancy school of yours?"

Libby couldn't help but grin. "Why, to always be discerning when it comes to a sizing up a gentleman, of course. With the occasional history and language

12

lesson thrown in for good measure."

"Well, just so long as they focused on the important things in life," her friend replied drily. She had a sense of humor that always made Libby laugh.

It was hard to imagine that they hadn't even known each other a year ago. After meeting at Libby's sister's wedding, they'd begun corresponding almost immediately. Since then, they'd written more and more prolifically, until Libby felt as though they had always known and loved each other. When Amelia had invited her along on her and Lord Winters's belated honeymoon, Libby hadn't hesitated to agree.

"Indeed. Didn't you know that finding a handsome, well-connected, deep-pocketed husband is the greatest goal in life?" Libby asked, batting her eyelashes in her best impression of the vapid debutante many expected her to be. A thought occurred to her, and she lifted a teasing brow. "Why, if you had attended, you would have been their greatest success story."

Amelia choked on a horrified laugh. "I shudder to think. I'm the least likely role model I can imagine."

"Nonsense. Who wouldn't look up to a viscountess with the aim of a champion marksman and the right hook of a prize boxer?"

Tilting her head, Amelia gave her an odd look before breaking out in a wide grin. "When you put it that way, I suppose I'm not the worst person in the world to emulate. Though it should be noted that my aim is vastly better than my right hook." Her smile wilted a little as her eyes darkened. "Every young woman should know how to protect herself *and* how to open her heart to the right man. In my opinion, both can be equally scary."

"I agree," Libby said with a decisive nod. "Although, at this exact moment, I am much more interested in the 'opening one's heart' part. As such, I see no harm in sharing a few words with a handsome stranger or two."

She'd spent her entire debut Season behaving with all the decorum that dreadful Uncle Robert and the school he had shipped her off to had relentlessly drilled into her. She'd smiled, she'd curtsied, she'd made polite small talk. It was good to know the proper way to behave, but she was positively itching to break a few rules.

Not the important ones, of course. She had no intention of finding herself ruined—or worse—by being imprudent, but a little flirtation here and there wasn't a sin, for heaven's sake.

Amelia shook her head, her expression teetering between amusement and exasperation. "It's comments like those that make me wonder how Lady Margaret ever convinced your uncle to allow you out of his sight."

Coiling a marigold ribbon around her fingers, Libby shrugged. "You know Aunt Margaret can be surprisingly persuasive when she puts her mind to it. And, of course, it did help that she could refer to my traveling companions as Viscount and Viscountess Winters when describing my plans to summer on the continent."

Amelia chuckled fondly. "She always was a clever old dear. Thank heavens she's feeling so well these days."

Nodding, Libby released the ribbon and went on to the array of satins. Aunt Margaret had been quite unwell in the months following Mama's death, but she truly seemed back to her old self these days. Which was a good thing since Libby had no intention of living with Uncle Robert, and she certainly didn't wish to impose on her sister Eleanor and her growing little family.

Behind them, the door to the shop creaked open, clanking the wooden chimes above the jamb.

"Pardon the imposition, ladies."

Libby's breath caught in her throat as she dropped the silky smooth satin she'd been caressing and wheeled around. The younger of the two Englishmen stood just inside the door, his blue eyes settled directly on her as he lifted his lips in that devil-may-care way that all the young Corinthians seemed to favor.

Before she could answer, his companion hurried in behind him, his face tight with displeasure. A flutter of excitement slipped through her chest like a ribbon caught in the wind. She'd wondered if she would see him again, and here he was, jarringly out of place among the cheery fabrics and ribbons.

He was probably only five or so years older than the other man, but the hawkish disapproval drawing his mouth taut and his brows together highlighted the discrepancies of maturity between the two. They had to be related, given their similar features and tall, lean builds. Oddly, despite his forbidding expression, something about the older man intrigued her. It had been such a kindness forfeiting those coins to the merchant, and he hadn't seemed to begrudge it at all. In a world where everyone seemed to pursue wealth like a religion, she admired that sort of generosity.

Forcing her attention back to the man who had

spoken to her, she lifted a single brow and said, "Have you need of an interpreter again so soon, kind sirs?"

"Actually," the young man said, meeting her gaze boldly as he stepped forward, "I was thinking exactly that. Not knowing anyone else in the city, not to mention another native English speaker, I thought it prudent to skip convention and introduce myself before the opportunity passed me by."

Amelia came to stand by Libby's side. Her lighthearted smile from earlier had disappeared completely and was now replaced with a suspicious frown. "And what, sir, would lead you to believe that the opportunity has not yet passed?"

"Excellent question," he responded, nodding once. "I decided to take a chance, madam. May I proceed?"

"*Nigel*," his companion hissed, warning tightly woven though the two harsh syllables.

"You see? It would seem my brother is eager to introduce me," Nigel quipped, completely unaffected by his brother's glare.

Amelia looked very much like a person about to refuse, so Libby quickly stepped forward. "But of course. Having an ally in a strange city is never a bad thing." She was less interested in the brash younger brother, but allowing his introduction would lead to learning the older brother's name.

"My thoughts exactly." Triumph warmed Nigel's eyes as he swept his hat from his head and bowed, causing his overly long brown hair to fall just so across his forehead. "Mr. Nigel Westbrook at your service." Straightening, he gestured over his shoulder toward his companion. "My older, wiser, and infinitely more boring brother, Mr. Philip Westbrook."

Though they looked quite similar, with their thick brown hair, dark-blue eyes, and perfectly straight noses, Nigel's face was still slightly rounded with youth whereas Philip's cheekbones and jawline were noticeably sharper. Truly, it was their expressions that set them apart from each other more than anything.

The elder Mr. Westbrook dipped his head in acknowledgment of the introduction, briefly smiling to both Libby and Amelia despite his clear displeasure at his brother. In fact, if she were to guess, she'd say at least some of the sharpness of his jaw came from the clenching of his teeth.

Libby held back a grin. She used to drive her own sister mad when they were younger and had been on the receiving end of that sort of look more than once. "A pleasure to meet you both. I am Miss Elizabeth Abbington, and this is my dear friend, Lady Winters. She is very disapproving of our appalling lack of decorum, in case you couldn't tell."

"Oh for heaven's sake," Amelia said, rolling her eyes. "You make it sound as though I am some prudish old matron, Libby. It is very nice to meet you both, but I do admit I think it best not to go introducing ourselves to every English-speaking stranger on the street. No offense," she added, offering a perfunctory smile that in no way resembled her actual smile.

"Noted and understood," Philip replied, the first hints of amusement curling his generous lips. "I attempted to impart exactly that concept upon my brother, but you see how successful I was. Not that I regret making your acquaintance, of course." His gaze slipped to Libby's as he spoke, sending a little frisson of awareness dashing down her spine.

Libby didn't shy from his gaze. Quite the opposite—she boldly returned it. She was here for adventure, was she not? "I'm so glad to hear it. Now that I have exactly doubled the number of people I know in this country, it is my hope that we might meet again." She purposely avoided looking toward Amelia. Chaperones—even those who were dear friends—were best no consulted when pushing the boundaries of propriety.

Nigel rubbed his hands together, the dove-gray leather of his gloves dulling the sound. "I can think of nothing that would please us more. An outing tomorrow, perhaps? With Lord Winters, too, I hope," he added with a nod toward Amelia.

She shook her head. "I'm sorry to say that he is tending to business for the next few days. We are in Spain in part because he's looking to invest in the refurbishment of the Royal Tobacco Factory."

Philip nodded, as though suddenly placing her. "He's the new viscount, is he not? I believe I recall reading about your marriage in *The Times* a few months ago."

Amelia's brows rose. "That's quite the memory, sir. Yes, he is."

"My congratulations to you both. From what I gather, the estate is better for having your husband at the helm."

Though he had no way of knowing it, Philip's words were exactly the right ones to lower Amelia's

18

defenses. All the better, as far as Libby was concerned.

"Well then," he said, smiling politely and backing up a step. "We won't keep you. My brother and I are staying at the *Augusto de Seville* for the month. If there is a time that pleases you to meet again, you've only to send a note."

Libby abruptly straightened. "The *Augusto de Seville*? Why, that's only two doors down from the house we're renting." Anticipation licked up her spine like a kindling flame. This little holiday just became much, much more interesting.

Though his smile didn't falter, something flickered in his eyes. Apprehension? Discomfort? Before she could properly read it, impassiveness took its place. "How fortuitous," he said, his voice perfectly correct and polite. "Then I look forward to the possibility of crossing paths. In the meantime, I wish you both good day." He tipped his head to each of them before turning and striding from the shop, leaving a vacuum of silence in his wake.

"Well," Nigel said, shaking his head as he stared after his brother. "I suppose that is my cue to leave you ladies to your shopping. I hope you'll forgive my brother; I'm certain he'll be much more agreeable when next we meet. Until then." He dipped in an abbreviated bow and took his leave.

After a few seconds, Amelia crossed her arms and turned back to face Libby. "Well," she said, clearly suppressing a whisper of amusement. "*That* was interesting. Remind me not to let you out of my sight on this trip."

Libby laughed, still getting used to her friend in

the role of proper chaperone. "I'll do no such thing. I will, however, promise not to do anything you wouldn't do."

Amelia groaned and shook her head. "Come along. I think I shall have Gabriel fashion a lead so I may keep you firmly tucked beneath my wing where you belong."

Waggling her eyebrows mischievously, Libby slipped her hand around Amelia's elbow and squeezed. "Mmhmm. We shall see about that."

The Westbrook brothers added a very interesting dimension to an already exciting trip. After the strict confines of her first Season this spring in London, it felt liberating to be free to simply talk to a man and not have people fret over his wealth, status, or connections.

Oddly enough, she had actually wanted to attend the annual pilgrimage to London and join in the unending rounds of parties, dances, and entertainments. Eleanor had warned her against joining their uncle and his wife for the Season, but Libby couldn't help but want to experience the right of passage, especially with so many of her friends from Hollingsworth attending.

It was a mistake she didn't plan to repeat.

Yes, the gowns had been gorgeous, the venues glamorous, and food amazing, but the novelty had very quickly worn off. All the posturing, preening, and outright deception of people of the *ton* had quickly tarnished the whole experience.

But this trip was something else altogether. There was no reason to hold back or pretend to be something she wasn't. She thought of Philip, and that instant spark of attraction when she'd first spoken with him. He certainly didn't have the overt charm of his brother, but he had shown kindness and a quiet authority that intrigued her. Hopefully Amelia would relax a bit when they next encountered the Westbrooks because Libby was quite determined: they *would* meet again.

Chapter Two

*"A*dmit it."

Philip glanced at his brother, wary of his smug grin. He'd been quite lost in thought as they'd navigated their way westward. The street had widened, and they now strolled along the pavement as carriages and wagons rumbled past. "Care to elucidate?"

"Elucidate?" Nigel chuckled, shaking his head. "Do you know, any normal person would have said *explain*. Or perhaps *clarify*. But yes, allow me to *elucidate*: you're glad I introduced us."

Directing his gaze to the mottled gray stones on which they tread, Philip gave a little shrug. "I am not sorry to have made their acquaintance. And it's good to know the viscount is staying near us. Fortunately, I've yet to meet him, what with his efforts to settle his affairs after inheriting the title and moving to England."

"Forget the bloody viscount. You know I'm referring to Miss Abbington. She's a tempting armful, if a bit of a bluestocking for my usual tastes. How many languages did she say she speaks?"

Five, if one included her rather polished, upper-class native English. And oddly enough, since he'd learned her Christian name first, he couldn't help but think of her as Libby instead of the proper Miss Abbington. It suited her. She was light and sweet, yet with an underlying intelligence that he found rather appealing. French, Italian, Latin, and passably good at Spanish? She was clearly talented.

A fact that had no bearing on either Nigel or Philip, since they hadn't come several hundred miles to be distracted by a woman.

Feigning disinterest, Philip shook his head. "I'm sure I don't know. However, she is obviously from a good family, so please do your best to use discretion when speaking to or about the woman. Actually, that applies to both women."

"Jesus, Philip, do you ever give it a rest?" There was real frustration in Nigel's voice as he threw up his hands. "We're in the middle of Spain, for God's sake—who are you worried will overhear? And more to the point, so what if they do? Thanks to your absurd insistence, no one knows who we really are, and even if they did, it's not a bloody crime to find a woman attractive."

The muscles in Philip's cheeks hardened as he clenched his teeth. His brother was missing the point. Their anonymity was meant to strip them of their preferential treatment; he hadn't expected for Nigel to look at it as a sort of carte blanche, enabling him to act any way he pleased without consequence. "I think we've gone far enough. Let's head back."

"Oh, would you look at that," his brother broke in, the words clipped. "A lovely little pub. Why don't you scurry on back to the inn while I soothe this parched throat of mine."

Squinting past the partially shuttered windows to the dim interior, Philip shook his head. "It is my understanding that public houses require funds, remarkably enough."

Nigel reached into his pocket and produced a palmful of coins. It was impossible to tell if his eyebrow was raised in challenge or triumph. "Then it's a good thing I stumbled upon a bit of blunt along the way." The metal pieces clinked as he jostled his hand before shoving them back into his pocket.

Exasperation speared through Philip like a blunted arrow. "Are we adding theft to your list of sins, then?"

"I consider it an advance on the money I'll collect at the end of this trip. Now if you'll excuse me, I find I'm suddenly in the mood for a little drink." Giving an exaggerated bow, Nigel turned and stalked toward the pub.

Philip blew out a long breath. Their first day in Seville had not gone at all like he had imagined. If he was going to get through to his brother, he had to stop reacting like a blasted governess and start acting like the concerned brother he was. Nigel was still impressionable. If he weren't, he wouldn't have lost a small fortune to that rat bastard of an earl, Lord Malcolm. From what Philip could gather, Malcolm had expertly manipulated Nigel, exploiting his youth and desire to be looked upon as his own man.

Not that Nigel hadn't been at fault, too. He was quickly gaining a reputation for fast living and hell-raising that Philip knew had to be nipped in the bud before his brother ended up just like their father. He had to tread carefully, though. Otherwise his brother would just dig in and refuse to listen to anything Philip said.

Pressing his lips into a thin line, he turned and headed back toward the inn. He'd let Nigel have his distance. In the meantime, perhaps it would behoove him if Philip could remember what it was like to actually relax for a moment.

***

Libby doubted she would ever get used to the beauty of a Spanish sunrise. From the vantage point of the fourth-floor balcony, she watched as soft orange light kissed the rounded clay tiles of rooftops all over the city. It was much quieter than London ever was this time of day, lending a remarkable peace for a place so densely populated.

"You're up awfully early."

She smiled over her shoulder to Amelia, who yawned as she padded toward the open doors. Her friend was still dressed in her nightgown and wrapper, with her hair gathered in a long braid that hung over her right shoulder. The bedchambers were on the third floor, but in the few days they had been here, Amelia had learned that the top floor balcony was Libby's favorite spot.

"I'm always up this early. You're the one who likes to sleep late," Libby teased as she turned and leaned her back against the black wrought-iron railing.

Amelia settled onto the small settee several feet away. Given her attire, Libby wasn't surprised that she didn't step outside. "Seven in the morning is hardly late. Certainly not by city standards." The sentence was punctuated by another yawn.

"Too true. But I am anxious to do some more exploring today. I thought perhaps we could see the cathedral first, as I am positively dying to see St. Ferdinand's tomb." Libby paused, quirking a brow. "That did not sound quite as I had intended."

Amelia laughed. "Fortunately for you, I know what you mean. Of course we may start there. I know how much you have been looking forward to it."

Biting her lip, Libby pushed away from the railing and went to join her friend on the settee. "I thought perhaps we could invite the Westbrook brothers to join us. They are quite the fish out of water here, after all," she added with an innocent smile.

"Uh-huh," Amelia said, lifting a knowing brow. "And which fish is it, exactly, that you are most concerned for?"

"I don't mind saying Mr. Philip Westbrook has quite caught my eye. But you needn't worry. I've no plans to husband hunt anytime soon. If nothing else, the Season taught me that. I merely think the added company would be good fun, and I'm happy to serve as translator for us all."

"My, what a generous offer," Amelia said drily, though her eyes sparkled with mirth. "Who am I to deny your services to our fellow countrymen? If you like, I'll have a note delivered to them."

Anticipation coursed through Libby's veins as

she clapped her hands together. "Oh, you are the absolute best. Thank you, and I promise I shall be on my very best behavior."

"Yes, please do. I'm quite the worst person in the world to be acting as chaperone, and I would hate to incur your uncle's wrath."

Libby made a face. "I know. Uncle Robert is a beast, but Aunt Margaret would protect us both." She had been quite the hero last year when Libby's sister had butted heads with Uncle Robert.

Amelia tilted her head. "Libby, my dear, you are quite missing the point. I don't wish to get out of trouble; I wish to avoid it."

Laughing, Libby held a hand over her heart. "I solemnly swear not to cause, find, or otherwise invite trouble for the whole of the time I am in your charge."

Lord Winters strolled into the room, his large frame expertly outfitted in a handsome gray jacket and buff-colored breeches. "I'm not sure I want to know what brought about that sort of promise," he mused, his deep voice liberally sprinkled with wry amusement.

Amelia smiled up at him, her whole visage brightening in his presence. "Libby wishes for an invitation to be issued to the Westbrook brothers for our sightseeing excursion today."

"The pair you told me about yesterday?" At Amelia's nod, he cut his dark gaze toward Libby. "They'd best behave themselves. If I know my wife, there will be a loaded pistol within reach at all times. And if I know myself," he added, his American accent thickening, "I'll be happy to introduce them to my fists should they step outside the bounds of propriety."

Knowing what she did about how the viscount broke nearly every rule in the book while wooing Amelia, Libby almost laughed. He was large and imposing, but she knew him to be quite the sweetheart beneath his scoundrel exterior. "My goodness, that was positively big brother-like of you to say. Completely unnecessary, but noted. And you are more than welcome to join us."

His chuckle rumbled deep in his chest. "That sounds much more agreeable than my day of meetings, but for some reason, they keep expecting me to attend."

"Then we shall tell you all about it tonight over dinner," Amelia said, coming to her feet to slip her hands in his. In this, they were much like Eleanor and her husband Nick. Little touches, stolen glances, knowing smiles—all the things that made Libby's eternally romantic heart happy.

***

That same heart was absolutely bursting with excitement hours later when the Westbrook brothers arrived. As Libby and Amelia came down to join them in the drawing room, Libby had to work to keep her enthusiasm at bay. Neither of the men seemed to hear them as they approached the open doorway. Libby's gaze flitted to Philip first. He stood tall and dignified beside the window, his hands resting behind his back. She could easily imagine him posing exactly in that manner for a portrait.

His brother, on the other hand, sat draped on the oversized chair dominating the back corner of the room. His hair was slightly mussed and pale-purple half-moons tinted the delicate skin beneath his eyes. He looked exactly like her cousin William whenever he stayed out carousing all night with his friends.

Philip noticed them first, turning away from the window with a polite smile already in place. "Good morning, Lady Winters, Miss Abbington. My brother and I are honored that you should think of us to join you today." His actual words were much more welcoming than the stiff way in which they were delivered. Nothing overt, but something about his precise enunciations spoke to some vague displeasure.

Nigel, on the other hand, grinned broadly as he came to his feet. "Ah, our rescuers. Good day to you both. I'm forever in your debt for your offer. Otherwise, I might have been stuck in the company of none but my brother the whole day, and I do believe that is a fate best not contemplated."

It was spoken in light, honeyed tones, but Libby could practically feel the tension between them. Had she been hasty in inviting two people she barely knew to spend so much of the day with them? She certainly hoped not.

"I might have said the same thing about my sister at some point," she replied, matching his tone. "No one loves or loathes quite like siblings."

She was relieved to see the glimmer of amusement in Philip's eyes. "Indeed, Miss Abbington. As the eldest of four, I can agree wholeheartedly with that statement."

Amelia shook her head. "As an only child, I can't speak with any authority about siblings, but I imagine it might be like having an opponent, coconspirator, and confidant all in one."

"Depends on your point of view, I should think," Nigel said, setting his hands on his hips. "As the youngest sibling, I was much less the confidant and much more the unwanted tagalong. Or more recently, the drag-along."

Libby glanced toward Philip, who was pressing his lips together. Yes, there was definitely some undercurrent between them again today. Wishing to diffuse it as best she could, she said, "Thank goodness such things are left behind in childhood. I am so grateful for my sister now that we are both adults."

Nodding briskly, Philip said, "As I am sure she is for you. Now then, shall we be on our way? I've heard that the cathedral can be quite busy during the day."

"Absolutely," she said, perking up at the mention of the cathedral. "I've been wanting to see it ever since Amelia's first mention of a sojourn in Spain. I'm particularly looking forward to St. Ferdinand's tomb."

For the first time that morning, Philip's face relaxed. "Ah, I can imagine why. For someone of your linguistic talent, a tomb inscribed with four languages must be something to behold."

As they filed from the room, Libby naturally aligned with Philip as they spoke. He held out his arm as they stepped outside, and she smiled and laid her hand along the superfine wool of his pale-blue jacket. She could smell the crisp, clean scent of his shaving soap, and as if of their own volition, her eyes darted to the smooth skin of his stubble-free jaw. For one mad moment, she imagined removing her glove and gauging the smoothness when her fingertips.

Drawing in a quiet breath, she nodded. "I've never even seen early-Castilian writing before, let alone heard it spoken. I'm only passably familiar with Hebrew and Arabic. But I am quite accomplished in Latin, so I am eager to compare the other languages to it."

From behind them, Nigel chuckled. "That's all well and good, but you do realize we'll be viewing a dead body, I hope."

Libby wrinkled her nose at the reminder. In theory, yes, she did know it, but it was less bothersome to simply imagine it was like visiting any cemetery or mausoleum. "It does sound quite ghoulish when you say it like that."

Philip's jaw tightened as he glanced back at his brother with narrowed eyes. Directing his attention back to the pavement in front of them, he patted her hand reassuringly. "Do feel free to ignore my brother, Miss Abbington. I fear he may have gotten his hands on a gothic novel or two whilst at Eton. I have every confidence the experience will be a good one."

She sucked in a surprised breath before belatedly covering the sound with a cough. She wouldn't have expected him to set his hand atop her like that. The weight and warmth of his fingers covering hers was deliciously welcome. "I'm sure it will be," she murmured, not daring to move her hand so much as an inch. If she were very lucky, perhaps he would leave it there.

***

Philip hadn't missed Libby's soft intake of air when his

hand had touched hers. It was a small thing, something he probably shouldn't have noticed, but for some reason, he was much more attuned to her than he should have been. He had noticed her sudden stillness, as well, and he'd allowed his hand to rest where it was, light enough that she could easily break the contact.

As furious as he was that his brother had accepted the invitation without consulting him, Philip could not bring himself to regret being by Libby's side just then. He had been determined to start anew with Nigel this morning, to set aside the contention of yesterday—of the whole month, really—and attempt to focus on the two of them.

He had purposely intended to discourage any more contact with Miss Abbington and the viscountess, knowing full well that Libby was far too interesting for his own good. Something about her had managed to slip beneath his normal disinterest in young misses. She was the perfect mix of irreverence, humor, intelligence, and beauty. Then there were the looks he had caught from her. Those were the most dangerous of all. She was interested, of that he was sure. Normally, that wouldn't mean anything to him, but on this trip, knowing that she had no idea he was a duke . . . ?

It was very heady, indeed.

His whole life he had been viewed through the lens of his title—even before he had it. As heir apparent, he already possessed the courtesy title of marquis, and there was no doubt of his eventual ascension. But with Libby, the draw between them was natural, unaffected by title, wealth, or position. He had felt it when they'd first met, and walking beside her now, there was no denying that the flicker of attraction was growing.

Unfortunately, it was also a distraction he feared would disrupt his efforts with his brother. Philip could almost see the man sliding into the persona Philip so disliked. The same persona that had already cost Nigel so much, thanks to the brashness it fostered.

Nigel had completely ignored Philip's stated instructions to politely decline any invitation they might receive from the ladies. When the missive had come this morning, Philip had been out exploring while Nigel had slept off the effects of the night before. He'd not hesitated to accept before Philip returned, knowing full well he was thumbing his nose at his brother by doing so.

Well, so be it. What was done was done, and there was no use allowing it to ruin the day. And truly, with Libby's slender form beside him, her light floral scent teasing his nose, Philip's annoyance was quickly evaporating. Since it was clearly not possible to avoid her company today, he might as well enjoy it. Perhaps in the process his brother could learn a thing or two about how to treat a lady.

As the four of them walked along, they chatted idly about their surroundings, the various shops, and even the weather. Despite the fact that it wasn't yet noon, the sun was already fierce, beating down on them with an intensity that was unlike anything they were used to. Though they stayed in the shade as much as they could, Libby was making use of the dainty pink-and-white parasol she had brought along.

"I can already tell I shall be covered in freckles by the time I return home," she said, her skin rosy in the pink-tinged shade. "My aunt will have a fit, but as far as I'm concerned, it's a small price to pay for the experience."

Philip returned her smile, grateful for the narrow pavement that made it necessary for them to walk in pairs. Nigel was several paces behind, engaged in conversation with Lady Winters about firearms, if he wasn't mistaken.

"I shouldn't worry overmuch, were I you. Freckles are one of those things women seem to notice much more than men."

"Hmm," she murmured, shaking her head. "Perhaps I should refer her to you when she rings a peal over my head about it." Her tone was lighthearted enough that Philip knew she wasn't overly concerned about it.

"Do you live with your aunt, then?"

Since she'd not mentioned her parents, it was a good bet that they were no longer around. A shame, given her youth. As far as he could tell, she was about nineteen or twenty. His own father had died when Philip was twenty-two, and even that was much too young to lose a parent, as far as he was concerned.

"Not quite." Her eyes settled on the pavement in front of them. "I've lived at Hollingsworth School for Young Ladies for much of the past two years. After that, I attended my first Season with my uncle and his wife, and now, well"—she shrugged, a small smile curving her lips—"now I suppose I live here. But when we return, I plan to join my Aunt Margaret at her home in the country. I love her dearly, but I'm not entirely certain I will survive the peace and quiet."

Had she really led such a transient life? It didn't sound as though she really thought of anyplace in particular as home. For someone as deeply tied to his ancestral home as Philip, the thought was sobering. Still, he made an effort to remain lighthearted. "So you are a butterfly, flitting from one lovely branch to the next."

She tilted her head as she glanced up to meet his gaze. Myriad emotions glimmered in her eyes, as though he had truly struck a chord in her. "I suppose that is exactly what I am," she said, a hint of sadness softening the words. She took a deep breath and smiled again, effectively shutting the door on the emotions he had glimpsed. "Although perhaps *moth* would be more appropriate. With my coloring, I'm positively monochromatic."

Surely she wasn't serious. Everything about her was luminous, as though sunshine followed her no matter where she went. "Monochromatic? Do you own a mirror, I wonder?"

"Yes," she exclaimed, giving his arm a light, playful squeeze. "A very good one, in fact. I can very clearly see dark-blond hair, light-brown eyes, and pale, yellowish skin. Not that there is anything wrong with that. It's just that I certainly don't possess the jewel-toned coloring that any self-respecting butterfly should, as you and Amelia do with your blue eyes. Or your brother, or my brother-in-law, and even my uncle—"

"All right," he said, chuckling as he cut her off. "So you don't have blue or green eyes. Instead you are in possession of golden hair, bronze eyes, and ivory skin. That makes your coloring far more valuable than mine."

"Oh, stuff and nonsense," she said with a very

undignified roll of her eyes. "But I thank you for the Spanish coin, sir, particularly given our whereabouts. Perhaps here it could actually buy me something."

He sent her a stern, ducal look. "I am a very busy man, under normal circumstances, and I have little time for flattery. I assure you, Miss Abbington, that you may take my compliments as the God's honest truth."

Her eyes widened a little at this pronouncement, and her already heat-reddened cheeks flushed a little deeper. "Well, then," she said, the words light with laughter. "I suppose I will say thank you and leave it at that."

"Wise woman."

The smile they shared was somehow private, despite the bustle of the streets around them. He held her gaze for a moment, savoring the warm tug of attraction between them.

"Miss Abbington," Nigel said, breaking the moment as he spoke up from behind them. "Lady Winters claims that if she managed to learn a little Spanish, there may be hope for me yet. Care to teach me a few lines before we reach the cathedral?"

Philip's disappointment was a physical thing, but he didn't protest. As much as it felt oddly right to be by her side, he had no claim on her time, nor she on his. Besides, his brother was at least behaving himself. Falling back, he allowed Nigel to step in front of him.

Whatever was building between Philip and Libby, it wasn't anything that could be sustained. Still, as he smiled at the viscountess and inquired about the conversation she had shared with Nigel, he couldn't help but miss the feeling of Libby's small hand on his arm or want to know more about how she came to be the butterfly she was. What had happened with her family? What was behind the sadness he'd seen in the honeyed depths of her eyes?

More importantly, why did he suddenly care so much to know?

Chapter Three

The cathedral was more magnificent than Libby could have ever imagined. It rose from the street in front of them like the monument to God that it was, seeming to span endlessly in all directions. The building was made entirely of stone, the sandy-colored blocks shaped into everything from rounded pillars to arching doorways to the great bell tower that rose hundreds of feet into the air. The tall, narrow spires reached toward the sky as the intricate balustrades and flying buttresses decorated the roof like the most sophisticated of layer cakes.

Still, even with one of the most spectacular structures in the modern world before her, Libby had a hard time focusing on anything other than the man standing so close to her. Scant inches separated their arms. During their walk, she'd seen a few more tantalizing glimpses of the man behind the polite reserve. That core kindness had resurfaced as he'd tried to soften the truth of her situation: she really didn't have a home anymore. She hadn't since the moment Mama had died almost two years ago, taking Libby's sense of home and belonging with her.

It wasn't something she liked to dwell on, and she loved that he had glossed over it to spare her feelings, even complimenting her in the process. There was something between them—she could feel it. The hum of awareness that skittered down her spine every time he drew near.

She'd always considered herself a romantic, but it was more that she believed in love, rather than having any sort of real understanding of it. She certainly had never experienced it. In truth, she'd never even felt like this before, as though her heart would pound right out of her chest at the mere sight of someone. It was . . . nice. Thrilling. Fun. Each time she felt the shimmer of anticipation at making eye contact, she immediately wanted to feel it again.

Leaning over just enough that the dainty cap sleeve of her gown grazed Philip's shoulder, she murmured, "Have you ever seen anything like it before?"

He shook his head slowly, his gaze traveling over the impressive roofline. "St. Paul's Cathedral is the closest I've seen, but even that is small compared to this. It's magnificent."

Libby grinned. "That was exactly the word I was thinking. I've seen St. Paul's, as well, and at the time, I thought it was spectacular. In fact, I'm glad I saw it first, so I could be impressed by both. I fear that had I seen it after I'd witness the grandeur of this one, I might have found it wanting."

Nodding absently, he said, "Indeed. What's particularly remarkable is how long ago it was built. I read only last evening that construction began in the early fifteenth century, and it took over a hundred years to complete. When the dome collapsed shortly thereafter, it took many years more to repair."

She turned to him and lifted an eyebrow. "Studying in our free time, are we? I'm not sure I took you for an academic." He didn't seem the type to pore over history books for fun. What he *would* do, she couldn't really say. Perhaps play chess or hunt. He just seemed like a man of action to her.

The smile that touched those beautiful lips of his was the most boyish she'd seen from him. Instead of denying her playful accusation, he appeared to embrace it.

"I'm an amateur at best. I strongly believe that we should never stop learning. There is so much to discover about our world, I can't imagine turning a blind, disinterested eye to it."

She stood up straight, surprised by his words. The thought of one of the pompous men she'd met in London saying such a thing was almost laughable. The fact that he felt that way only served to highlight how mismatched she was for those men of rank her uncle had repeatedly pointed out to her.

"I feel exactly the same way! It's why I study languages. I want to spend the rest of my life learning as many different ones as I possibly can."

"Is that why? I assumed it was simply easy for you."

She scowled at him, mildly offended. "While I'll

admit I have a predisposition for it, it certainly isn't easy. It's a challenge, though one I relish. But my reasons go beyond that. The idea of speaking to people all around the world, with no barrier or interpreter diluting the experience, is absolutely thrilling."

He shifted his position, turning away from the spectacle of the cathedral to face her. His blue eyes glinted in the bright sunlight as he met her gaze. "Do you know, I never thought much about learning another language. I hadn't intended to travel abroad, so it didn't seem necessary. I did study a little French, but honestly, I think I only chose that in case I ever happened upon some dastardly French spies and needed to warn the government of their plans."

She laughed out loud, gaining the attention of several passersby, not to mention Amelia and Nigel, who were inspecting the intricate designs of the massive front doors. Libby grinned sheepishly before turning back to Philip. "How patriotic of you."

"Such were the thoughts of an imaginative twelve-year-old boy. I could have been hailed a hero, you know." He nodded sagely, not a hint of humor to ruin the effect.

She could just picture him as a young boy, full of thoughts of saving the world. "Well, I'm sure there's still time. You never know what the French are up to."

"You may have just read my mind," he said, crossing his arms. The movement brought attention to the broadness of his chest, momentarily distracting her. "That aside, after being here, I'm realizing just how big the world is past the shores of England."

Amelia walked toward them then, with Nigel

trailing along behind her. The younger Mr. Westbrook looked somewhat worse for the wear, with a sheen of sweat dampening his forehead and highlighting his pale complexion. The purple smudges beneath his eyes still remained, making her wonder again just how late he had been out the night before—or if he'd slept at all.

Amelia tugged on the brim of her hat, adjusting the angle to better shade her eyes. "Are we quite through with admiring the exterior? As glorious as it is, I'm ready to get out of this sun, even if it means visiting tombs in order to do so."

"With enthusiasm like that," Libby replied drily, "how can I refuse."

Slipping her arm beneath Libby's elbow, Amelia gave her a completely innocent look. "I'm more than happy to leave you here to roast, if it pleases you. I'm sure Mr. Westbrook would be delighted to keep you company."

For some reason, a blush rose up Libby's cheeks. She didn't mind being a little bold, but she didn't wish to be obvious. "I've waited weeks to lay eyes on St. Ferdinand's tomb. By all means, let us proceed."

As they made their way toward the massive double door, Libby couldn't help but gaze up at the incredibly detailed stonework above the arch. Truly, it resembled nothing so much as filigree and fine lace. How on earth had the masons managed to create such a delicate design out of stone?

With her attention focused upward, she paid no attention to the stone surface beneath her feet—until she tripped over an uneven seam. She gave a little squeak of alarm as she pitched forward but came to a jarring stop as Philip caught her by both arms. The supple leather of his kid gloves was like a second skin against the bare expanse of her upper arms. Her heart thundered at the feeling of being held in his arms, making her momentarily dizzy.

He carefully brought her back to her feet but didn't drop his hold right away. "Are you quite all right?"

She cleared her throat once, then again, before managing to find her voice. "Yes, of course. Thank you. I really should pay attention to where I'm walking."

Dropping his hands, he stepped back. "Normally, yes, but it seems to me that this entire cathedral is designed with the sole purpose of making a person look up."

"Yes, exactly. Obviously my clumsiness is entirely the fault of the builder's poor planning some four hundred years ago."

Chuckling, he held out his elbow. "Allow me to escort you, then. Consider me your guide as you take in the splendor around us."

Libby didn't hesitate. If he was offering contact, she wasn't about to pass up the opportunity. Together, they crossed the threshold into the hushed darkness of the central nave. It took a moment for her eyes to adjust to low light, but when they did, she tightened her grip on Philip's forearm.

"It's beautiful," she breathed, almost too overwhelmed to take it all in.

The ceiling soared above, easily six or seven stories high. The stone pillars lining the length of the nave were as wide as century-old oaks, sweeping up into graceful arches where they met the ceiling. And oh, what a ceiling it was! Nearly every inch seemed adorned in some decorative design or another. The effect was as though she were standing beneath a domed blanket of gray and gold lace, so light and airy it was impossible to believe it was really stone.

Libby's gaze swept down the walls. There were statues, paintings, and the most wonderful stained glass that sent prisms of colored light dancing across the marble floor. Not a single nook or cranny was overlooked, so no matter where she turned, there was something spectacular to see. Interestingly, much of the interior seemed to shimmer as if plated in gold. She froze, her eyes widening. "It *is* plated in gold," she whispered.

"Indeed, it is," Philip whispered back, bending his head close to hers so she could hear him. Despite the fact that mass was not in session, the place still inspired reverence. "Or to put a finer point on it, it's covered in gold leaf. I thought you would have known that."

She sent him a sheepish grin. "I'm afraid I was too enthralled with the tomb to pay much attention to anything else when I was reading about it."

Nigel and Amelia stood several paces ahead of them, quietly taking in the dark, warm interior. At Libby's comment, Nigel averted his gaze from the ceiling and lifted a brow in her direction. "Then by all means, Miss Abbington, we should go there directly. I've never been one to delay gratification."

Since her hand still rested on Philip's arm, she could tell the moment his muscles tensed. Why did he always seem so disapproving of his brother? He was a bit of a scoundrel, but at least he was charming. Truly, he had the sort of attitude that came a penny a dozen in the beau monde.

Smiling at Nigel, she said, "Yes, let's. Sometimes it can be fun to go straight to dessert."

The four of them proceeded deeper into the cathedral, all the while marveling at the exquisite architecture and craftsmanship. When they reached the tomb, for a moment none of them said a word. Libby stared in awe, astounded by the incredible gold and silver metal work and equally shocked to discover that the saint's body was on display, encased in a crystal casket.

"On second thought," Amelia said, as though continuing a running conversation, "I think I'll go wait somewhere else." Grimacing, she turned and hurried from the alcove.

Libby exchanged glances with Philip, guilt weighing her conscience. "I should go with her. I didn't expect to actually *see* the body. She might be unsettled by the sight."

Nigel gave a little snort, causing both Libby and Philip to turn toward him.

"Apologies. I was just recalling the rather detailed discussion we had on the merits of different pistols. She may not wish to stand here and ogle the dead man, but I doubt she was terribly upset by it."

Philip glared at his brother, widening his eyes as though to convey a message. "Nigel, please."

"What?" he replied, all innocence. "We all know it's a dead man. I see no reason to dance around the bush. In fact, I'd say he looks pretty damn good for his age."

Abruptly pulling his arm from Libby's grasp, Philip stalked forward and put a hand to Nigel's back. "If you can't show a bit of decorum, I suggest you go elsewhere while Miss Abbington reads the inscriptions. I'll thank you to remember that we are in a church."

"Yes, a *Catholic* church," Nigel retorted. When Philip advanced another step, the younger man held up his hands. "Fine, fine. I'm going."

Philip waited until his brother was halfway to the center of the church before turning back to Libby. His features were taut, his eyes somewhere between anger and defeat.

"He does know how to get under you skin, doesn't he?" Libby said, offering him a sympathetic smile. "If it helps, I don't think he's specifically attempting to annoy you."

Sighing heavily, he shook his head. "Sometimes yes, but most times no. Things have just been a bit tense between us lately, and I am attempting to work things out with him. My apologies if it has leeched any of the joy from this excursion from you."

"No, of course not," she said quickly, shaking her head for emphasis. "I rather like your company. I hope we'll be able to enjoy several more outings together while we're here."

His grim features relaxed at her words, and he came to stand by her side. "I enjoy your company, as well, which is why I insist that you get on with what you came to do." Gesturing dramatically to the letters carved into memorial next to the tomb, he said, "Now, tell me with this says."

Smiling at the thrill of hearing him say he liked spending time with her, she forced her attention to the task at hand. Each of the four sides of the tomb were inscribed with a different language. She circled slowly, admiring the careful lettering of each. The Castilian, Hebrew, Arabic, and Latin translations were beautiful in their own right, easily competing with the gold and crystal that vied for the observer's attention.

She paused in front of the Latin version, the language at which she most excelled. The letters were crowded into the small plaque but were still legible. Smiling, she stepped forward and started to read.

***

From several feet away, Philip watched Libby run her fingertips reverently over the etched words as she read. Did she even know her lips were moving? He doubted it, but he found it rather endearing. Her brow was knitted in concentration, and he took advantage of her distraction, allowing his eyes to roam her petite form.

From this angle, he was treated to a view of her long, slender neck, which was angled slightly to the right. His gaze followed the smooth line of her jaw, the curve of her ear, the delicate bow of her collarbone where it disappeared beneath the shawl she had draped over her shoulders. Swallowing, he stepped forward and murmured, "What does it say?"

Her eyes flicked to him, and she smiled briefly before returning her gaze to the inscription. "Bear with me, for the wording is a little odd and I'm not quite sure of the names, but here is my best translation:

47

"This place is the tomb of the great king, Don Fernando, master of Castile and Telitala, and Leon and Valesia and Asvila and Karteva and Murcia; and who lives his life in heaven; who captured all of Spain; the right; the justified; the pius; the humble who feared God and worked for him all his life; who broke and destroyed all of his enemies and honored all those who loved him; and who captured the State Asvili, which is the head of all Spain, and died there on Friday night, twenty second day of the month Sivan, of the year five thousand and twelve from creation."

Philip nodded, his eyebrows lifted. "Well, the man certainly puts me to shame. That's quite an impressive epitaph—no wonder he became a saint."

Libby chuckled and shook her head. "Of all of that, I am most impressed that it shall forever and always be known that he died on a Friday night. How wonderfully specific."

She circled around to another side, her lips pursed. "And here it is in Hebrew. Did you know that both Arabic and Hebrew are read and written from right to left? It makes me wonder if it was invented by people who favored their left hands for writing."

"Either that or they had a fondness for inkstains on their wrists," Philip mused idly, his attention once again captured by her profile. It was a very nice profile, one worthy of being immortalized in a minuature. It was unfortunate that she hadn't a parent or beau who might have use for such a thing.

"Mmm," she murmured noncommitally, her eyes tracking back and forth over the letters. "I rather wish I would have brought some paper to do a rubbing.

I'm facinated with the characters they use to form the Hebrew alphabet. It looks so different carved in stone compared to any printed version I've seen."

"Perhaps we can return later, then." The words were out of his mouth before he'd even realized he was going to say them.

She looked over, meeting his gaze, a smile gracing those beautiful lips of hers. "I think that sounds like a fine idea."

Once again, he found himself meeting her smile with one of his own. Yes, he was here for his brother, and yes, he needed to concentrate on that, but with an entire month to spend here in Spain, setting aside a bit of it for Libby sounded eminently agreeable right about then. "Excellent. Now then, shall we go rescue Lady Winters from my brother?"

She nodded and slipped her fingers onto the sleeve of his jacket, bringing the scent of jasmine with her. "Thank you for joining us today. I doubt the experience would have been nearly as memorable without you."

Philip didn't tell her that he felt exactly the same way.

Chapter Four

"*A*re you absolutely certain you don't mind going to the church alone today?" Amelia still seemed unsure, despite the three other times Libby had assured her it was fine.

"For the last time, yes. And I won't be alone; I'll have Colleen with me." Libby smiled brightly as she gathered up her parasol, reticule, and lightweight shawl. The maid already waited beside the door, hints of excitement bleeding through her normally staid expression. Turning her attention back to Amelia, Libby added, "Salvador wouldn't be nearly as interesting to you anyway—not after having already seen the cathedral."

"I admit I'm not overly excited about the prospect of seeing another old church, but that doesn't mean I wouldn't be happy to accompany you later in the week."

Amelia had been a wonderful companion this

trip, but the truth was, Libby was looking forward to a little time to herself today. Shaking her head, she said, "No need. You and Gabriel enjoy your day together. I'll look forward to hearing your thoughts on the *Real Fábrica de Tabacos* building over supper tonight. It's not every day a husband wishes to have his wife's opinion on his investments, after all."

Libby paused to check her reflection in the mosaic-framed mirror hanging above the small table in the entry. "And for the record," she said, sending a teasing grin toward her friend, "I do find it ironic that, of all places, you'll be visiting an area referred to as *de las calaveras*."

Amelia met her gaze in the mirror, suspicion creeping into her sapphire eyes. "And why is that?"

Twisting around to face her directly, Libby said, "After your reaction to the tomb earlier this week, I wouldn't think an ancient Roman burial ground called 'of the skulls' would be your location of choice." It was something she'd stumbled upon last evening while browsing through one of her books about the history of Seville. *Calaveras* had been a word she hadn't known until then.

Instead of the reaction Libby expected, Amelia broke out in a sly grin. "Oh, Libby, did you truly believe I was squeamish about that? I must be a more accomplished actress than I realized."

Libby gaped at her. "What on earth are you talking about? Of course I did! Whyever would you feign such a reaction?" She knew her friend to be quite clever, but devious? That was a surprise.

Looking very pleased with herself, Amelia lifted

her shoulders in a breezy little shrug. "I may be a chaperone, but I'm not the prude you take me for. I saw the spark between you and Mr. Westbrook. I was merely facilitating a bit of private time between the two of you."

Libby could hardly believe what she was hearing. She laughed out loud, delighted that her friend would do such a thing. "You may very well be my favorite chaperone ever. And here I thought you wished to keep me tucked beneath your wing."

Amelia grinned. "It occurred to me that if your uncle could encourage you to dance, stroll, and talk with men the whole of the Season, I could certainly allow for a little of the same here, right?"

"Absolutely," Libby said with a definitive nod of her head. "Especially since Mr. Westbrook is vastly preferable to any of the men I met in London." Perhaps that explained why she had been thinking of him so much this week, hoping they would run into him every time they left the house. It was a bit of a disappointment that she'd not heard from him since their trip to the cathedral, but it had only been four days.

After sharing a tight embrace with her friend, Libby set off for the church, Colleen in tow. It was another exceptionally warm day, and she was glad she had worn her most lightweight summer muslin, a pretty white frock with delicate mint-green leaves embroidered on the hem. She felt light and summery and exceedingly happy as she made her way down the street, listening to the rapid-fire Spanish being spoken all around her.

It was fun to try to translate the snippets of conversation in her head. A woman purchasing flowers, a man calling out his wares, a shopkeeper shouting across the street in greeting to a friend—it was all simply life as usual. That was one of the greatest things about learning different languages. Without the barrier caused by lack of understanding, it's possible to see that people from other cultures are still just people.

She paused at an intersection, looking right at the exact moment that the man to her right looked left. Her heart dropped to her stomach as her gaze collided with Philip Westbrook's.

"Mr. Westbrook!" Her voice came out as a high-pitched squeak, and she paused to clear her throat before continuing in a more reasonable tone. "And Mr. Nigel Westbrook—how wonderful to see you both."

Her heart fluttered madly as she turned to face them fully, trying very hard not to stare at Philip. He was even more handsome than she'd remembered, with his newly sun-bronzed skin making his blue eyes stand out in stark contrast.

He smiled easily, looking genuinely pleased to see her. "Miss Abbington, you're looking very well today. How are you?"

Pleasure whispered through her at the compliment. "Quite well, thank you. Although I fear this heat has marked me with a permanent blush." She could have bit her tongue. She knew her cheeks were brighter than ever, but the excuse only called attention to it.

Nigel lifted an eyebrow, mirth stretching his lips. "Never mind the heat, Miss Abbington. A man likes to think a lady's blushes can be attributed to his presence."

Unsure of what one was supposed to say to such a thing, she smiled a little too brightly. "Well, I admit I am quite pleased to run into you. How has your week been? Enjoyed anything of note since last we met?" Her eyes naturally went to Philip, wondering if he had thought of her as much as she had of him these past few days.

Nigel gave a humorless little chuckle. "*Enjoyed* is too strong a word by half," he said, his tone momentarily putting her in mind of the insolent young bucks she had met during her Season. "*Endured* may be more like it."

"Oh no," she said, her brows coming together. "Have you not had the opportunity to explore the city?"

"On the contrary. My brother has dragged me all over this city, attempting to force the merits of the culture. A dreadful bore, all of it."

Philip's shoulders stiffened as he cut his eyes toward Nigel. "Yes, it's my insidious plan to attempt to have an enjoyable holiday in the company of my brother." Though the words were spoken in a light, bantering tone, an undercurrent of exasperation was definitely there.

Tipping his chin up, Nigel said, "Well, perhaps you can enjoy the company of another for awhile. Miss Abbington, you appear to be without your usual delightful companion. Could I impose upon you to rescue me from an afternoon spent gazing upon musty old paintings?"

She inwardly cringed at the comment, knowing it wasn't really in jest. He had to be about her age—certainly not yet twenty. How was it he seemed so much more immature than she? Charming one moment, petulant the other. The Westbrook family must have quite a bit of wealth behind it for him to act like some sort of entitled Corinthian.

Although, it was interesting that Philip was almost his polar opposite: polite, courteous, and gentlemanly to a fault.

Except perhaps when it came to his sibling. It was clear that he would have dearly loved to give a proper dressing down, but instead he straightened and said, "If you wish to spend the afternoon in your own company, Nigel, then be my guest. Miss Abbington needn't abandon her plans on my account."

In that moment, Libby's heart went out to him. No one liked to think his company was intolerable. And when it came to Philip, such a description couldn't be further from the truth. The thought of spending the day by his side, with no chaperone beyond the quiet presence of her maid, was enough to send a fluttering wave of butterflies through Libby's stomach. *Breaking the rules, indeed.*

Mind made up, she turned to him. "'Musty old paintings' wouldn't happen to be referring to the *Museo de Bellas Artes*, would it?" Given their location, it was a pretty good bet.

The clouds cleared from Philip's eyes as he quirked a brow. "Assuming that means the Museum of Fine Arts, then yes, that was where I was headed."

"Well, how fortuitous," she said, smiling brightly as though she wasn't about to lie through her teeth. "As it happens, I was just headed that way now."

***

The interior of the old building that housed the museum

was surprisingly light and airy given its age. As they stepped into the main entryway, Philip glanced around, taking in the impressive mosaic tile murals that greeted them. The lower half of the walls were completely covered in bold, abstract designs featuring brilliant blues, reds, yellows, and teals. The upper half featured several religious-themed mosaic portraits that stood out against the whitewashed walls, creating a striking effect, especially given the soaring height of the ceiling.

An attendant greeted them, speaking a flurry of Spanish in a deep, resonate voice that echoed pleasantly in the open space. Philip waited as Libby spoke to the man, taking the opportunity to peer past the tall, arched doorway into the yawning space beyond. The building was much larger than he'd originally thought.

He listened as Libby spoke, not understanding one bit of it but enjoying the way her tongue wrapped around the words. Despite his annoyance at his brother for forcing the pairing, Philip had to admit it was a relief to spend the day with Libby instead. No matter how hard he tried to bring Nigel out of his moodiness, his efforts only seemed to push him away. It was like trying to touch a rainbow: the more he advanced, the farther away it seemed.

If he was honest, he was beginning to suspect that his brother actively resented him. Was it possible that Nigel was jealous of Philip's title and the coffers that came with it, or that he begrudged the fact that Philip, as head of the household, had the right to tell Nigel what to do?

Whatever it was, he was tired of dealing with it. Having Libby by his side was a vast improvement to his day, even with the rather unseemly way it had come about.

Concluding her conversation, Libby turned her attention back to Philip. "He said that the most popular part of the collection is located upstairs, but he suggests we start downstairs and make our way up. There are three separate courtyards that he says aren't to be missed, the largest of which is straight back and to the right."

The golden glow of her lovely eyes was like a balm, draining any residual anger at his brother from his system. He nodded, not really caring which way they went, and offered her his elbow again. The light fragrance of jasmine drifted on the warm air as she stepped close and slipped her hand over his arm. They started off, the light tap of the maid's footsteps following a discreet distance behind them.

They paused in front of the first painting they came to, a canvas nearly as tall as he was, depicting angels and cherubs lounging blissfully among clouds in the sky. Interestingly enough, it bore a striking resemblance to the mural painted on the library ceiling at his estate in Gillingham.

Sighing happily, Libby smiled. "I could look at something like this for days."

"It is rather peaceful," he said, thinking of the hours he had spent beneath his own mural at home. His great grandfather had commissioned it some sixty years ago, and it was said to have taken almost a year for its Italian artist to complete.

"*Peaceful* is exactly the word. I love how it feels as though you could just reach out and touch the clouds.

Aunt Margaret and Uncle Robert both have extensive art collections, but they consist mainly of dark portraits and boring, bucolic paintings of the countryside."

He had his share of those, as well, but with the exception of the portraits of his father and grandparents, he rarely paid attention to them. "Are you saying you'd have something different in your own home?"

"Absolutely," she said without hesitation. "First of all, any painting I'd own would be full of color and light, not dark and moody. I'd have paintings of places I hope to visit, and perhaps some of the places I've been. What good are pictures of a countryside you can see right out the window?"

"Excellent point." They moved on to the next painting, which depicted Madonna sitting on a throne with the baby Jesus in her lap and saints at her feet. Angels peered down from the clouds above, but this time the mood was more somber. "I wonder, what are some of the places you would like to visit?"

She held out her hand and began counting down on her fingers. "Rome, Paris, Florence, Zurich. Possibly the Greek isles. I've heard the Mediterranean Sea is absolutely beautiful."

"That's quite a list. Will you regret it if you aren't able to visit them all?" As a duke, traveling like that had never really been an option. His place was in England, where he could see to all of his vast responsibilities.

She shook her head slowly, her lips pursed. "No, I don't think so. But I've always felt it was good to have dreams. To aspire to more than you could ever possibly accomplish. If we had everything we want in life, then what would be left to strive for?"

It was an interesting point of view. So many people believed if they could just have enough money, or a lofty enough status, then they could be happy. As someone who had one of the highest titles in the land and one of the vastest estates—even with all the work it was taking to return it to its former glory—he knew that those things couldn't bring contentment. He'd often wondered why his father had seemed so desperately unhappy and had turned to things like gambling and drinking.

Libby's words really resonated with him. What if his father hadn't had anything to strive for? What if having everything he could want in his lap had robbed him of any real enjoyment in life? Maybe that's why he'd seemed to develop such contempt for it by the time he'd died.

They continued on, stopping at a few more paintings before coming upon the open door that led to the largest of the courtyards. Glancing around the nearly deserted, surprisingly lush gardens, he said, "Would you like to explore outside? It might be best to do so before it gets too warm."

"Yes, absolutely. It looks like the Garden of Eden out there."

She was right. It was like a secret garden, lush and verdant in the middle of a city, unseen beyond the museum's two-story tall walls. They strolled beneath the red-painted arches of the breezeway before choosing one of the small gravel paths. Swiveling around, Libby smiled at her maid. "Do feel free to relax on one of the benches on the perimeter while we're out here, Colleen.

It's a small enough space that we should be able to see each other."

The maid nodded and found a seat, leaving them in relative seclusion. Philip breathed a sigh of relief. Finally, a bit of privacy.

As they walked beside a fragrant copse of neatly pruned orange trees, Libby trailed her fingers along the waxy leaves of the nearest branches. "Did you know that this building was built in the sixteenth century and used to house a convent?"

"I did not," he answered, looking around at the architecture with new interest. "I suppose that's not surprising, given the style."

She nodded. "It's so peaceful. It's not hard to imagine an order of somber women going about their prayers and duties here. Perhaps that has something to do with the large number of religious works here."

"Are you an admirer of religious art, Miss Abbington?" It was an idle question, but he was content to speak of idle things just then. For the first time in days, he was truly enjoying himself. The air wasn't yet too hot, the grounds around them were extraordinarily peaceful, and the woman beside him was so perfectly easy to be with.

"I would say not particularly, but given our recent outings, it would appear that I am. I suppose it can be said that I am an admirer of beautiful things, and the Roman Catholics certainly excel at producing such art."

He could have easily said some clever turn of phrase about her beauty outshining anything around them, but here, it didn't seem necessary or expected.

Instead, he simply nodded and continued on, content to be in the company of such an interesting and intelligent women.

It occurred to him then that they hadn't once had the typical banal exchanges so common when men and women conversed. She seemed to have no need to hide her light under a bushel, so to speak, as so many of their class were taught to do. God forbid a man might somehow feel inferior if a woman sounded cleverer than he did. Absurd notions like that were what kept him from joining in the beau monde's endless entertainments.

Well, one of the many reasons.

"Indeed, they do," he agreed. "I've actually wondered if the Vatican is as impressive as they say. It's hard to imagine anything outshining the cathedral here."

"I know exactly what you mean. Of course, the ancient Romans managed some pretty spectacular feats of engineering several millennia ago, so it stands to reason the more recent accomplishments of the region would be the same."

He cut his gaze to hers, surprised. "Do you know Roman history, as well? In addition to all the languages and the history of Spain and England?" She had said she wanted to go to Rome, but it had seemed more of a general desire.

Her smile spread as she shrugged. "When I'm taken by a language, I'm taken by the history of its people. I want a feeling for the places it was spoken and developed in order to better understand the passions and struggles behind it. And I hope that doesn't make me sound completely mad."

"On the contrary—it makes you sound completely brilliant. You must come from a rather remarkable family, to encourage that kind of learning."

She paused in front of the bubbling fountain, her smile still in place but sadness seeming to tug at her features. "My mother encouraged us to pursue what we loved. She and my aunt believed in independence and the importance of thinking for ourselves."

Libby bit her lip for a moment, looking over Philip's shoulder to a place he knew he wouldn't be able to see, even if he turned around.

"Your mother sounds like an extraordinary person." It was as close to prying as he would get.

She nodded, her ever-present smile subdued. "She was. Mama died almost two years ago, and I miss her every day."

"I'm sorry for your loss. My father died three years ago, and though we had a difficult relationship, I still think of him often." Just because his father made decisions that drove Philip mad, he still loved the man. That was the way of it with family: despite the turmoil, blood would always be thicker than water.

Libby's amber eyes found his as her fingers gently tightened on his arm. "I'm sorry. It's harder, I think, when the relationship was troubled. I can assure you, if he could see the man you are today, he would be proud."

Her quiet assurance surprised him. She knew so little about him, yet she said the words with such conviction, he could almost believe they were true. "I'd like to think so, but I doubt it. My brother is just like him. I should have known we were destined to butt

62

heads. He just can't see that I am attempting to save him from the pain the path he's chosen will bring him."

He'd never said anything so private to anyone before. He knew to be on his guard at all times, lest someone find a weakness to exploit. But here with Libby, where he wore the insulating cloak of anonymity, he was free to be himself. Though he claimed a false name, he was being more honest than he'd ever been in his life.

"I think it is the burden of the oldest to want to save their younger siblings from whatever strife they foresee. The problem is, we don't always want to be saved. Sometimes a person has to make mistakes for himself before the lesson can sink in. And sometimes," she said, sending him a rather mischievous glance, "it doesn't turn out to be a mistake at all. Despite your best intentions, you may not always know best."

He made a show of looking offended. "Nonsense. I'll have you know that I am never wrong."

"Then I'm not certain we can be friends," she quipped, arching a golden brow. "I do so hate a know-it-all who *thinks* he's always right." She started to tug her hand away.

Before he'd even had a moment to think, Philip reacted, covering her hand with his own and pressing it tight against his sleeve. All he knew was that he didn't want to break the contact, or forfeit even an iota of the intimacy, between them.

With his heart suddenly pounding in his ears, he met her startled gaze, forcing a small smile to his lips. "Then I take it back."

Chapter Five

*L*ibby's stomach dropped to her toes at the look in Philip's eyes. She couldn't have turned from him for anything, nor could she have tugged her hand away. She nodded slowly, her mouth suddenly dry. "All right then," she murmured, her voice breathy even to her own ears. She swallowed before trying again, this time working to infuse a teasing note into her words. "I suppose we can still be friends."

Even as she said it, *being friends* was the very last thing on her mind. At that exact moment, she was thinking of what it would be like to be kissed by this man. To feel his arms wrap around her and pull her tight against him. To hold her breath as he lowered his lips to hers and to learn for herself if he tasted as good as he smelled.

His sudden earnestness had called to something deep inside her. She may be young and properly chaste, but she'd seen a real kiss before. She'd seen the way passion could ignite, consuming a couple so thoroughly that the rest of the world ceased to exist. It was something she yearned to experience, even if she knew such a thing would be breaking the rules outside of a proposal, at the very least.

But wasn't she here to break a few rules?

Oblivious to her thoughts, Philip flashed a smile that made her heart pound all over again. "Excellent. I should be bereft without my interpreter." Patting her hand, he started forward, leading them around the back of the fountain and onto another path.

Rallying her wits, she managed to give a little laugh. "Somehow I doubt it. You have the sort of personality that shall persevere, no matter what."

"That's a rather sweeping statement to make about someone you've only known a week."

"Time matters less than instinct when assessing one's character. I don't need to spend months with you to know you'll always land on your feet. Where are you from, Mr. Westbrook?"

He blinked, apparently taken off guard by her change of topic. "Er, Gillingham. East of London."

"All the way from Gillingham, east of London, to Seville, western Spain. You don't know the language or a single person here, yet you've managed to get around quite well. *That* is the spirit of a man who knows how to make things happen."

He chuckled, shaking his head a little incredulously. "Well, if I know how to persevere, you know how to follow through. I'm in awe of the dedication it must have taken to learn so many languages. I imagine you could do anything you set your mind to."

Warmth infused her limbs, as if stepping into a freshly drawn bath. "I do believe that is the finest compliment I have ever received. Thank you."

"It is the truth, Miss Abbington. And I hope you never allow anyone to tell you otherwise."

Libby thought of her uncle and the disapproving frown he wore whenever she was near. She thought of the teachers and tutors who had frowned upon her desire to study more than the bare minimum, as though learning too much was as disagreeable as eating too much. There had been the men who had frowned when she'd spoken of anything outside of the weather and fashion, and women who had clucked their tongues and told her she should close her mouth and open her ears if she wished to attract a man.

Looking down at their feet, she noted with pleasure just how close together they were walking. Her smile was slow and completely natural when she looked up and met his gaze once more. "I don't plan to."

His answering smile was soft and sincere. "Good."

The rest of the afternoon was absolutely delightful. They talked the entire time, their heads bent together as they toured the gardens and the rest of the museum. When they could linger no longer, they headed back to where they were staying, stopping along the way to purchase a few small gifts for Philip's two other siblings. He had stood back and allowed her to haggle with the vendors, cheering for her when she managed to save him a bit of money.

When at last he bid her farewell and she climbed

the stairs up to her chambers, she couldn't help but laugh when she realized she couldn't recall a single painting or sculpture from their entire time at the museum. As far as she was concerned, he was, without a doubt, the most interesting thing there today.

***

Early morning was not typically Philip's favorite part of the day, but here in Seville, it was fast growing on him, thanks to the cool morning air that blanketed the city, bringing much-needed relief from the ever-present heat.

This morning, as he walked back from his daily trek to the waterfront, he found his mind was focused on one thing, and one thing only: Libby.

All he could think about was when he might be able to speak with her again. It was disconcerting, really; he'd certainly never been so preoccupied with a female before. He was still far too busy getting the estate where it needed to be. Father had left things in shambles, and Philip had spent years sorting it out. Things were certainly beginning to turn around, but there was no room in his life just yet for a bride.

He'd had one person after another approach him about a seemingly beneficial marriage match—always more beneficial for them than Philip—but he had absolutely no interest. Not with so many other things on his plate, and particularly not with the way things stood with his brother.

Yet despite all that, he found that he was smitten.

Here, in this city of warmth and beauty, so far away from the cool and levelheaded life he had always known, he was smitten with a woman who didn't even know his real name. He was taken with a girl who had absolutely nothing to gain by being with plain Mr. Westbrook. She had shared her heart with him, and he with her. Not in the way of lovers, but in the way of people with a soul-deep connection.

He'd only be here for a short time, and he wanted to explore that connection more. What if there could be something beyond the shores of Spain? It was a thought that both thrilled and terrified him. What would she think of him if she discovered he was a duke? Surely it would be welcome news. Yes, he was deceiving her, but it wasn't as though he was hiding something terrible. If things progressed and he decided they would suit, he could approach the truth as a happy surprise.

An odd, charged thrill raced through him, making his heart kick in his chest.

This changed everything. He needed to come up with a way to see her again—hopefully with some amount of regularity. After all, he only had three weeks remaining, and he intended to make the most of it.

***

Hours later, Philip sat smiling blandly at Lady Winters over a small glass of lemonade—it was entirely too warm for tea—as Libby pressed her pretty lips together as though attempting to suppress the pleased grin that lifted the corners of her mouth. His request had obviously had the desired effect.

The viscountess, on the other hand, blinked several times, her confusion abundantly clear. "I beg your pardon, Mr. Westbrook, but you would like to do *what*?"

"Hire Miss Abbington to help convert my rusty French into some basic Spanish. I underestimated the difficultly of being in a foreign place without knowledge of the language, and after a week of bumbling around like a fool, I'd like to do something about it."

The idea had come to him in a flash as he had been walking home. After their conversations on the importance of always learning, it seemed the perfect, if wildly unconventional, excuse to spend more time with her. Libby had a passion for languages—what better way to enjoy each other's company than by tapping into that passion?

"I . . . see," Lady Winters responded lamely, sending a sideways glance to Libby. "I must say, that is a most unusual request. In fact, I believe we can safely call it unseemly."

Libby straightened her features as she met her friend's gaze. "What is unseemly about a gentlemen wishing to improve his mind and his circumstance? I'm rather impressed that he would wish to undertake such a task."

"Perhaps," Lady Winters said, even as she shook her head. "However, I believe your uncle might very well kill me if I allow such a thing. A lady cannot accept payment for anything, let alone dabble in actual work."

"Excellent point," Libby said, her amber eyes sparkling as she nodded solemnly. "Obviously I could never charge a friend for simply helping him to learn a few pertinent phrases. However, I am more than happy to donate my time to such a worthy cause. In fact, I think it would be great fun."

Philip almost choked on a laugh. Was she calling him a *charity* case? Still, the fact that she was so eager to go along with his plan buoyed his spirits tremendously. "What a generous soul you are, Miss Abbington. I would be eternally grateful should you decide to honor me with your talents."

"Of course, Mr. Westbrook. I'm flattered you should think me capable of helping you." She was the very picture of innocence, smiling at him like that.

Lady Winters glanced back and forth between them, clearly undecided as to what to say. From what he'd observed, she may be acting as chaperone, but she was a friend, as well, so it was impossible to predict what she would decide. "I don't know. How would such a thing work?"

"I am a firm believer that the best way to learn a language is to immerse oneself in it. Perhaps Mr. Westbrook and I should take a daily promenade—with Colleen in tow, of course—and we could start by translating the signs, the shops, and naming common objects in the marketplace."

The viscountess pursed her lips. "Perhaps we could simply call it a walk, then. Surely your uncle wouldn't object to a walk?"

"Of course not," Libby said firmly. "He sent me on at least a dozen walks and carriage rides with gentlemen of the *ton* this Season."

Looking somewhat relieved, Lady Winters nodded. "It's settled then. Though I do think two or three times a week at most would be prudent. When would you like to start?"

Philip allowed a pleased grin to come to his lips.

"I'd like to spend the rest of the day with Nigel, but are you free tomorrow morning? Perhaps before the temperatures rise too much?"

"I am, indeed. Is ten o'clock acceptable? A little early by English standards, but it should still be quite pleasant at that hour."

Already, anticipation coursed through his veins at the thought of having her to himself again. "Perfect. I shall see you then."

Chapter Six

*L*ibby could scarce recall a time when she had been more excited. It was a simple enough thing—taking a walk while teaching a bit of Spanish—but the outing wasn't what was so thrilling. It was the fact that Philip had purposely sought her out. He'd as good as announced to her that he enjoyed spending time with her and wanted to do so more often.

And she felt exactly the same way.

As they started off down the street, he smiled that lovely smile of his as her fingers rested on the familiar perch of his forearm. "Good morning," he said, the word much warmer than the polite greeting they had shared when he had arrived at her door earlier.

She looked up into those soulful blue eyes of his and smiled. *"Buenos días."*

He chuckled, the sound sliding over her like velvet. "And so it begins. Very well. *Buenos días.*"

"Very good," she said, nodding approvingly. "I

think you shall be an *excelente* study, *Señor* Westbrook."

"Ah yes, I do so like the words that match English so closely. And for the record," he added, pulling her just a little closer to his side, "*me llamo* Philip, if you please."

Her brow lifted as she glanced up at him in surprise. "Breaking the rules, are we?"

"I merely thought it would be easier when we are together like this. After all, I am your pupil, no?"

Was he teasing her? If so, she was more than happy to play along. "Indeed, you are. But I'm not sure I want to be Miss Abbington if you are Philip, even if I am your teacher."

He led them around a stand of citrus fruits that partially blocked the pavement before answering. "Then Libby it is."

She loved the sound of her name on his lips. The only men who ever called her that were her cousins, Nick and William. With them, it was ordinary, but with Philip? A sweet shiver ran down the back of her neck. It was perfect.

They spent the next half hour wandering through the market, walking just a little too close together as she pointed to fruits and vegetables, buildings and people, patiently naming each in Spanish. They both knew it was a pretext, but if it could keep her by his side, than she was happy to keep it up.

He was absolutely terrible at the language, though, and comically mangled the pronunciations as he repeated after her. She laughed frequently and happily soaked up his easy smiles and teasing scowls.

"You are a very good sport, Philip," she said

when he'd joined in her laughter after he'd tried to pronounce *pájaro* when she'd pointed to a gull flying overhead.

"No, not terribly. I'm normally boring and serious and unwilling to play games. I think you bring out a side of me that is usually dormant. I think that's one of the reasons I like you so well."

Pleasure at his words curled through her, making her heart give a little flip. "I'm glad that I can do that for you. Ironically, I like *you* so well for almost the exact opposite reason. I feel the most free to be myself around you. I absolutely hated the feeling that I had to guard every word I said during the Season. It was so terribly stifling."

He nodded, his eyes serious. "I know exactly what you mean. Having to constantly police one's words is exhausting."

She slowed, turning to face him. "Have you attended the London Season?" She had assumed it was outside of the world he operated in. She'd never seen him before, and heaven knew she'd attended a thousand events this spring.

Something chased across his features, but it was gone before she could name it. "I've been to a few events in the past."

"Really? I wonder if we have acquaintances in common and we didn't even know it." Was it possible that they could cross paths again in the future? This time in England, where real life awaited them in a few short weeks. It was a thought that had hope bubbling up in her chest.

"Hard to say," he said, giving a one-shouldered

shrug. "Luckily for us, we've no longer need for an introduction." He offered her a small smile before glancing down to his watch fob. "Unfortunately, I fear our time is up for today. I am feeling much more accomplished in my *español* skills, *señorita*. *Muchas gracias*."

She grinned at his pathetic attempt to roll the *r* of *señorita*. "*De nada*. Shall we meet again the day after tomorrow?"

He gave her a slow, private smile that made her pulse flutter. "I'm looking forward to it."

***

The Spanish lessons may have very well been Philip's best idea to date. After two weeks, he may only know marginally more Spanish than when he'd started, but he had enjoyed every minute by Libby's side, idly walking the streets of Seville, listening to her talk about her childhood, her time at Hollingsworth, and a bit more about her abysmal time in London with her decidedly unpleasant-sounding uncle.

Their time together had made the whole trip worthwhile, which was a good thing, seeing how he had made little progress with his brother. Nigel still acted as though Philip was doling out cruel and unusual punishment by bringing him here. The play they had attended last night—Shakespeare, no less—had been a resounding failure, and Nigel had accused Philip of attempting to kill him with boredom. Philip had snapped that Nigel's tastes simply ran to the baser things in life, which hadn't gone over well.

"I'm not sure I want to know what you're

75

thinking."

Philip blinked and glanced over to Libby. "I'm sorry?"

She offered him a gentle smile, her eyes golden in the morning light. "You're in quite a brown study over there. I thought you said you enjoyed visiting the waterfront."

Grimacing, he said, "My apologies. I'm still having some issues with Nigel."

"I'm sorry to hear that," she responded, empathy wrapped around the words. "It's such a shame that things seem so difficult between you. Has it always been like that?"

He shook his head, staring out over the water. "No, not at all. When he was young, he practically worshipped the ground I walked on. He followed me like a shadow, and *most* of the time, I loved having him there."

"Most of the time?" He could practically hear the smile in her voice.

He chuckled, remembering his outrage at discovering his little brother hiding in the bushes during Philip's first kiss. "A young man doesn't always want his baby brother around."

"Ah," she said, nodding in understanding. "That much I understand. Eleanor nearly killed me the day she found me reading her diary. It was the last time she ever wrote in it, as far as I know."

The breeze kicked up, sweeping a few strands of her blond hair across her face. Without thinking, he reached up and brushed it aside. His knuckle lingered at the curve of her cheek for a moment too long before he dropped his hand to his side.

She moistened her lips, her chest rising and falling with the sudden quickness of her breath. God, what he would give to have a moment truly alone with her. There were so many times he had thought about touching her, so many times his gaze had settled on those beautiful lips of hers and wondered exactly what they would feel like beneath his own.

Attempting to reclaim his wits, he glanced back to where her maid sat at a bench overlooking the water, and when he looked back to Libby, she seemed to understand the subtle reminder.

Taking a small step away, she said, "So what happened then? With your brother, I mean. Did you simply grow apart?"

All of the ardor of a moment ago fled as he remember the circumstances that had changed everything. "My father died. He"—Philip hesitated, searching for a delicate way to say his father had been caught in bed with another man's wife—"made some very bad choices that resulted in being challenged to a duel. He rather foolishly accepted, though for the life of me, I cannot figure out why."

Philip considered it over the years, and the only explanation he could come up with was that, as duke, his ego had inflated to the point that he felt he was both infallible and invincible. He couldn't have been more wrong.

"But . . . it's illegal," she stammered. "Even if he'd won, he would have gone to jail."

He shook his head, unable to explain his father's conceit. He also couldn't very well tell her it was extraordinarily improbable that a duke would have ever been charged. The problem would have likely magically gone away, just like all of his father's other problems with the law.

She blew out a breath, her eyes full of compassion. "I'm sorry. That must have been a horrible time for your family. I can see how it might have taken a toll on your relationship with your brother."

If only it had been that easy. Pressing his lips together, he met her compassionate gaze. "My brother was fifteen at the time. For reasons I still don't understand, my father laughingly named my brother as his second. Thinking nothing would ever really hurt our father, Nigel agreed. He was witness to the whole thing." He could still remember his brother's ashen face when Philip had rushed home after receiving word of the tragedy.

Libby's gasp pulled Philip from the darkness of the memory.

"I'm sorry," he said, regretting his candor. He'd never told anyone about that day. A peer of his stature did not air the family secrets.

Shaking her head, she closed the distance between them and placed a gentle hand on his arm. "Please don't be sorry. I just hate that your brother and your family had to go through such needless pain."

He nodded. "It was a difficult time. My mother and I handled Nigel with kid gloves after that, wanting to compensate for the trauma of it. Unfortunately, it has recently become abundantly clear that we did him no favors."

Even so, Philip still didn't know what he would

have done differently. It's hard to imagine punishing a boy for acting up when he had been through so much.

Libby tilted her head, considering him. "In what way? He's a bit of a scoundrel, to be sure, but he's doesn't seem to mean any real harm."

If only that was the extent of it. Philip rubbed a weary hand over the back of his neck. "He's fallen into a downward spiral, it would seem. He's becoming more and more like our father every day, which worries me, for obvious reasons. With his brash attitude, he seems to think he is invincible, just like our father once did. Unfortunately, that sort of arrogance makes one an easy target to those with no scruples."

Her brows scrunched together. "What do you mean?"

Fresh anger welled up at how his brother had ruined himself, especially knowing he still hadn't learned his lesson. "The truth is, the entire reason we are here is because he recklessly bet a small fortune— money he didn't actually have—on the turn of a card. I brought him here with the hope of straightening him out. None of the old distractions, no privileges, no wastrel friends to encourage his behavior. Unfortunately, I seem to be failing."

She was quiet for a few moments, staring off at the deep-blue water of the harbor. "How can you fail at something that really isn't in your control?"

His eyes snapped to hers, surprised at the softly spoken words. "What do you mean?"

Turning to face him fully, she regarded him with more seriousness than he had ever seen in her. "We can't always be responsible for another person's choices. You can show them the right way all you want, but in the end, they are free to choose their own path—for better or worse."

He blinked a few times, processing her meaning. It might make sense for another, but he was the duke, damn it. It was his responsibility to care for and guide those under his protection. He shook his head, unable to accept what she was saying. "I can't give up on him. He's my only brother, and I can't allow him to fall to ruin."

Her smile was sweet enough to make his heart ache. "I never said give up on him. I only meant that you do what you can, but in the end, a person's destiny is up to him. If he's determined to fail, then you might have to let him. But Nigel is your brother. No matter what, I hope you never give up on him."

The words echoed in the part of his heart that had been hollowed out by his inability to help or change his brother. He turned them over, examining them, testing them. What if he never could help Nigel? What if he could never force him to stand up and act like a man? Could Philip release the burden of his brother's destiny, even as he continued to try to help him? It was a possibility he hadn't considered, one that felt somehow freeing.

Turning his attention fully back to the woman in front of him, he slipped his fingers beneath the hand she still rested on his arm. Slowly, purposefully, he raised her hand to his mouth and pressed a featherlight kiss to the supple leather of her kid glove. "How ever did you get to be so wise, sweet Libby?"

As he watched, her eyes darkened and her breath

hitched, making his heart pound. Drawing a slow breath, he turned her hand over, exposing the delicate, nearly translucent skin at the inside of her wrist. Lifting her hand once more, he touched his lips to the soft warmth of her bare skin. The smell of jasmine teased him as he closed his eyes for the space of a second. *Bliss.*

Releasing his hold, he straightened and smiled at the lovely woman he'd come to admire so much. "Forgive me. In a place as beautiful as this, with a woman as lovely as you, sometimes it is easy to forget oneself. I'm beginning to think this place holds a bit of magic, making the rest of the world seem far away."

Her smile seemed to light her from within, like sunshine through a jar of honey. For a few moments, neither of them spoke, content to simply be there together. Philip watched as boats went by in the harbor, from huge ships to little fishing vessels. The sound of the water lapping at the shore, the soft scent of the woman beside him, the feel of the sun warming his shoulders—he couldn't remember a time that he had ever felt more content.

"This is my heaven," Libby said, breaking the silence between them.

"What, the Seville harbor?"

"Not exactly," she replied, throwing him a little grin that hit him square in the chest. "But it reminds me of all the things I want in life. The sea, a small cottage, the smell of the salt-tinged air, the magic of the pink-hued sky . . ." She trailed off, and he couldn't help but wonder if he fit into that picture at all.

It occurred to him then what she'd been describing: a small, quiet life. He'd never known anyone, most especially not a young lady of the beau monde, who didn't wish for the biggest and best house money could buy, located at the most enviable address. "You'd rather have that than a massive estate somewhere, throwing balls and dinner parties and wearing the very best fashions from Paris?"

He tried to picture her in a sophisticated gown with her hair coiled into some elaborate coiffure but couldn't. To him, she was simple muslin gowns and straw bonnets and sun-kissed cheeks.

"Oh, I shall always be fashionable," she quipped, her eyes dancing with a sweet playfulness. "But if experiencing my first Season has taught me anything, it is that life without the pomp and circumstance is vastly preferable."

He couldn't hide his incredulity. "Are you saying you don't wish for a titled husband?" It seemed as though that was the goal of every young miss on the marriage market. Something very close to disappointment settled in his gut.

"God, no." The two words were quick and decisive on her tongue. "I'd rather be wed to a fish monger than an earl or duke or some other such nonsense. With the exception of Amelia's husband— who I should point out most certainly had no expectation of becoming a peer—every titled man I have known in my life has been arrogant, self-important, self-serving, or downright disagreeable."

He blinked, surprised at the vehemence with which she spoke. "And for the sake of argument, how many would you say you've actually met?"

Her grin was swift and unrepentant. "Oh, I met

scads of them this spring—"

"Scads?" he repeated, interrupting her with a grin. "Is that like a peck or a bushel?"

Laughing, she shook her head. "All right, I'll admit to having met a few perfectly decent lords during my foray into society. But I've seen the life they lead outside of the glittering ballrooms. My uncle's life is one of dreary responsibility and the singular pursuit of greater wealth and prestige."

"I thought everyone wanted riches and power. Isn't that what we all wish for?" He was genuinely curious. His status and holdings had been assured from the moment he was born. He had always known he would have power and wealth.

"Freedom is not to be had in either of those things. The more we have of each, the more we are slaves to them. I want the freedom to actually enjoy my life."

Once again, he was taken aback by her astuteness. "Such sage wisdom from one who is so young."

"One doesn't need to be old to have wisdom. It is observation that makes us wise."

Sharing a smile, he almost dropped the subject when he suddenly realized what she had said about her uncle. "Wait a second, you said your uncle's life. Is he a *peer*?"

For some reason, the thought had never occurred to him. Yes, she had spoken of her Season a couple of times, but he had assumed she was on the outskirts of it all. And honestly, somewhere along the way, he had gotten the impression that her uncle was a social climber.

She grimaced and nodded. "Unfortunately, yes. He's an earl, actually, and is not exactly a shining example of the peerage."

Uncle Robert. The first fingers of dread slid down his neck as all humor fled. "Libby, who is your uncle?"

He suddenly wished he could freeze the moment, stopping the words that he knew, simply *knew*, would be coming.

"Oh, I hadn't considered that you might know of him. He's Robert Ashby, Earl of Malcolm."

The very man who had purposely set out to ruin Philip's brother.

Chapter Seven

The change in Philip was almost instantaneous. Libby's brows came together in confusion as she watched his jaw harden into a harsh line and the light drain from his blue eyes. She reached out, setting her hand against his elbow. "Philip, what is it?"

Because, without a doubt, it was something. Libby knew full well that there were those who disliked her uncle. He'd had no qualms about using his position to bully people. Had he somehow hurt Philip?

He shook his head, pulling his arm away. "I think we need to get back. We've been gone far too long." His voice was wooden, devoid of the warmth she had come to expect.

"No, please. Something is wrong, and I want to know what it is." She felt suddenly cold, despite the sun that still shined down so brightly it almost hurt her eyes.

His expression remained stony. "It's nothing. Call your maid, and we can head back."

He started to walk around her, but she stepped to the side, forcing him to acknowledge her. "Quit acting like I am some sort of child. Obviously I've upset you, and obviously it has to do with my uncle. Tell me what it is."

The muscles of his jaw worked as if he were grinding his teeth. "Your uncle is not a good man."

She gave a humorless laugh. "Yes, I know. He's been better recently, but—"

"*No*, he hasn't. If anything, he is worse than ever."

Oh, God. Swallowing against the tightening in her throat, she said, "Tell me."

Philip was silent for a moment, focusing somewhere over her shoulder. When he met her gaze, there was a barrier between them that hadn't existed before. "Your uncle wanted something from me. When I refused, he threatened me, saying I'd regret it. When I held firm, he made good on his promise by setting out to ruin my brother."

She gaped at him for a moment, trying to make heads or tails of what she was hearing. Philip knew her uncle? Her uncle had threatened him? Worst of all, he had actually set out to harm Nigel? "I-I don't know what to say. I'm so sorry."

She felt as though a pit was opening up between them. Philip looked so distant, so oddly detached, it squeezed her heart to know he was pulling away.

"It is not yours to be sorry about," he answered, his tone even and polite. "If you are not ready to leave, I understand. I'm certain you and your maid know the way back."

And just like that, he turned and walked away, leaving her staring after him. As she watched him go, the hurt flowed into her chest, filling the place where happiness had resided only minutes earlier. In that moment, she realized exactly how much she had come to care for him.

Somehow, someway, she had to find a way to make up for what her uncle had done.

***

"Where the hell have you been?"

Philip's fury was so complete, he didn't even try to temper his voice as he stood in the entry of their suite of rooms with his fists planted on his hips and a fierce scowl contorting his features. What had happened yesterday with Libby had been utter hell. Returning home to an empty apartment hadn't helped things. But waiting up all night for a brother who had as good as vanished had taken Philip to his breaking point.

His brother's timing could not have been worse. Walking away from Libby yesterday had been one of the most difficult things he'd ever done. But damn it all, it was best to step away while he still could. He'd been falling for her, hard and fast, and it wasn't until that moment that he'd realized how much.

But he had to walk away. He couldn't allow himself to be with the very girl Lord Malcolm had tried to entice Philip to marry. *Elizabeth.* It never occurred to him to connect that bastard's niece with the smart, sweet woman he had come to adore.

After Malcolm had swindled Nigel out of so much, Philip would be damned before he gave the man what he wanted all along: marriage to his niece.

And now the other player in this tragic little farce had finally shown up. Seeing him now, walking in with stubbled cheeks and a devil-may-care attitude, brought in equal parts relief and fury. As much as Philip could kill his brother right now, he was still relieved Nigel wasn't injured, missing, or worse.

"Good morning to you, too, brother," Nigel drawled as he unbuttoned his jacket and slid it off. As he tossed it on the table next to where Philip stood, the pungent odor of alcohol and tobacco filled the air between them.

Philip gritted his teeth with the effort of keeping his temper in check. "That's right—*morning*. One should be waking, not going to sleep. And you didn't answer the damn question."

"Because it's none of your damned business," Nigel shot back as he tugged at the knot of his cravat. The thing was stained by some unknown amber substance, a disgrace to any self-respecting gentleman.

"I'm your brother and, at present, the keeper you've repeatedly proven you've needed," he said, his staccato words spoken through clenched teeth. "If you remember, I hold the blunt that will save you from drowning in the River Tick. If you wish to continue to live in the manner to which you're accustomed, I suggest you behave according to my rules."

Nigel snorted, the sound harsh and angry. "How the hell could I possibly forget? You've lorded the fact over my head for a month now. The agreement was that I accompany you here and refrain from revealing your identity—both of which I've done. If you want someone to obey your every command, I suggest you hire another servant or get a bloody dog."

His brother breezed past him and stalked to the small dining table. He selected a peach from the bowl in the center and took a large bite, not seeming to care that juice dribbled down is chin and dripped onto his stained cravat.

Philip raked his hands through his hair, biting back the desire to resort to fisticuffs with the man. "I don't know why you are so damned determined to act like you are some sort of martyr, unfairly persecuted by your unreasonable and boorish older brother. I don't expect anything from you that I don't expect of myself. For the love of God, have a little respect for others."

Narrowing his bloodshot eyes, Nigel swallowed and said, "Well, that makes sense. Why wouldn't a duke, who is in control of a vast fortune and all the power and privileges the title brings, expect his worthless younger brother with no title and pockets to let, to live up to the same standards?"

Philip drew back, stunned by the vehemence with which his brother spoke. "There are standards of conduct no matter who you are. And might I point out, all that power and wealth you spoke of comes with tremendous responsibilities. My life isn't some sort of stroll in the park."

Letting out another snort, Nigel threw him a disgusted glare. "Oh yes, so difficult you could barely find the time to jaunt off to bloody Spain for a month."

Before Philip could form a response, a commotion arose in the corridor. Metal scraped against metal before the door flew open, banging against the wall behind it. Both Philip and his brother sprang to their feet, gaping at the four men who poured into the room, shouting a flurry of Spanish words. Philip recognized the innkeeper, but the others where unknown to him.

He held up his hands trying to stop the chaos around him. "What is the meaning of this?" he demanded, his voice strong enough to cut through the commotion.

The men advanced into the room, and it suddenly dawned on him that they were all armed in one capacity or another.

"*Senõr* Garcia, explain, please." But the man just shook his head, gesturing to the others as they grabbed hold of Nigel roughly.

He desperately tossed about for the right words and tried again. *"Explicar, por favor."*

Holding up his hands, he said the one word that Philip could understand: *hermandades*.

All the air seemed to whoosh form the room as Philip staggered back a step. Dear God, these men were with the municipal league.

Nigel was under arrest.

Chapter Eight

*S*itting on the fourth-floor balcony of Lord Winters's rented townhouse, Libby had noticed Nigel stumbling up to the inn where he and Philip were staying and had watched as he disappeared inside. It was early enough that very few people were up and about, so she had also noticed when three very purposeful men had strode in a few minutes later.

Not that she had given them much thought. She was far too absorbed in her own heartache to give anything other than idle notice to the men. But minutes later when the trio reappeared, dragging a protesting Nigel along with them, she bolted to her feet, her heart lodging in her chest. What the devil was going on?

She ran inside, shouting for Gabriel as she thundered down the stairs. She was grateful she was already dressed, but it wouldn't have mattered if she wasn't. This was Philip's brother, and he was in trouble.

By the time she rushed outside, her lungs heaving with exertion, the men had made it to the street with him and were trying to stuff him into a waiting carriage.

"Wait!" she shouted, then promptly switched to Spanish. *"Detener!"*

To her surprise, they actually stopped, gaping at the sight of an Englishwoman running toward them, her hair streaming down her back and her cheeks surely bright red.

It was then she saw Philip, rushing up behind them with wide, nearly panicked eyes.

"Philip, what's happening?" she asked, panting.

He shook his head quickly. "I don't know. I can't understand them, and they won't stop. Libby, it's the *hermandades*."

Her heart dropped to her knees. What would the notoriously brutal civil police want with Nigel? There was only one way to find out. Lifting her chin, she stalked over to them, holding her trepidation at bay. Searching for the right Spanish words before she spoke, she said, "Gentlemen, what business have you with my friend? What are the charges?" Though her voice shook, her gaze didn't waver.

They exchanged glances, obviously unsure what to do with her. At last, the tallest of the three shrugged and spoke curtly in Spanish. "He is a thief, miss. He stole a precious jeweled ring."

A thief? Nigel? It was an absolutely absurd claim. What use would he have for a ring? Turning to Philip, she translated the charge.

"It's a lie," Nigel shouted, struggling again. "I didn't steal anything—I *won* it."

As fast as her brain could translate, Libby conveyed Nigel's claims of innocence to the *hermandades*. The words were met with out and out hostility as the men sneered back at her. "Of course he'll not admit to it. All thieves are liars," the tall one said, clearly in charge. The hard glint in his dark eyes chilled her from the inside out.

Again she translated, her heart going out to the look of panic in Nigel's eyes. He shook his head, his gaze boring into Libby's. "I won it, I swear. I beat his hand fairly."

"What's going on here?"

The sound of Gabriel's booming voice made Libby nearly wilt with relief. His not inconsiderable presence helped even the odds. She quickly relayed the situation. Crossing his arms over his barrel chest, he turned to address Nigel. "Where is the ring?"

"In my inner jacket pocket, upstairs in the room. They can have the bloody thing."

The lawmen looked to Libby, and she hastily repeated Nigel's words. One of them turned to the innkeeper and directed him to retrieve the jacket.

As the man hurried inside, Philip took a cautious step closer to his brother. "Nigel," he said quietly, his eyes dark with intensity. "Are you telling the truth?"

Pain darkened Nigel's already bleak eyes, and Libby's heart broke for him. "*Yes*," he croaked. "I took money from your satchel when you were gone, and I used it to go gambling at the hall near the pub. I swear to you, I won the ring. The man who lost it was furious, but I took it anyway and came home."

Philip nodded once, then stepped back, keeping a wary eye on the *hermandades*. The innkeeper reappeared a moment later, an ornate gold ring pinched between his forefinger and thumb.

Nigel seemed to sag in relief. "Take it. Just take it," he said, his voice cracking.

The lead lawman inspected the ring, nodded, then tucked it into his pocket. *"Vamonos,"* he said, tipping his head toward the carriage. The other men nodded and started to drag Nigel into the carriage.

"What are you doing?" Libby cried in Spanish, rushing forward only to be caught by Gabriel from behind.

"Careful," he murmured, clearly mistrustful of the men.

"This man has just produced the evidence of his guilt," the officer who had taken the ring said, his expression obstinate. "He must face his punishment."

Libby gasped, and Philip stepped forward. "What the hell is going on? What did he say?"

She hastily repeated the words, all the while racking her brain for how she could stop the men from taking Nigel away.

Laying a heavy hand on her shoulder, Philip spun her around and looked her dead in the eye. She'd never seen him more serious or determined. "He's not guilty, and I won't have him treated as such. Tell them I will pay them whatever they want, but to unhand him this instant."

But when she did as he demanded, the words had no effect whatsoever. The two men continued to pull Nigel toward the waiting carriage, while the driver sat in his box with the reins in hand.

The leader sent a condescending smirk toward Libby before saying in Spanish. "He cheated the wrong man this time." Turning his back, he started up behind his men, obscuring Nigel from view.

Heart pounding, Libby grabbed Philip's bare hand in her own and translated the man's parting words. For the space of a breath, they shared a glance that was soul deep, moving past the quibbles of the day before. She could *feel* his dread, just as she could see the determination solidifying in his eyes. Flexing his jaw, he squeezed her hand and whispered, "Forgive me."

Before she could grasp what on earth he meant, he broke away and turned to face the enemy, pulling himself up to his full height. Shoulders back, nostrils flared, and chin lifted he looked every bit as regal and imposing as a Roman general.

"*Alto!*" he demanded, his voice echoing down the street like a clap of thunder. Everyone froze—the *hermandades*, the innkeeper, even Libby and Gabriel. He seemed bigger than life, powerful and compelling in a way that made it impossible to look away.

Stepping forward, he pinned the lead lawman with a razor sharp glare. "By order of the Duke of Gillingham, Marquis of Cuxton, and Viscount Westbrook, I *demand* you release my brother, or I swear to you this incident will single-handedly jeopardize this country's trade with England for the next fifty years."

All at once, the world seemed to slam to a jarring halt, robbing Libby of breath and comprehension. Her head swam as she stared at Philip—her Philip—who had transformed right before her eyes. Gone was the kind, gentle, laughing man she had known, and before her stood a man of steel, radiating enough power and command to put even Wellington to shame.

Eyes wide, the *hermandades* shifted their attention to her, cautiously waiting for the translation. Philip turned and met her gaze, begging, *commanding* her to pull herself together and speak.

Slowly, as though moving underwater, she turned to the men and struggled to translate the words that her mind rebelled against. How could he have lied to her? How could he have let her fall in love with him, knowing it was all a ruse?

When she finished speaking, the men looked back and forth between them in stunned silence, clearly weighing his words. Even Nigel looked stunned, lying limply in the *hermandades's* hands as he gaped at his brother.

After what seemed like hours, the men nodded to one another and shoved Nigel away, sending him stumbling to the pavement below. They quickly closed the door and rapped on the ceiling, and just like that, they were gone.

Libby stood staring after them, unable to turn and face the man who had so thoroughly made a fool of her. All this time she had been falling for a man who didn't exist.

"Libby." Philip's powerful voice was reduced to a hoarse whisper.

She shook her head, valiantly fighting against the tears that threatened to humiliate her even further.

"Libby, please. Let me apologize. Let me explain."

She held up a hand, the movement jerky. When she was sure she could speak without dissolving in tears, she turned to face him, her chin held high. "Consider our families even."

With that, she marched past the duke, his brother, and Gabriel, past the stunned innkeeper and the handful of people who had come to stare, and all the way inside.

If she had thought her heart was broken before, she now knew what it was to be crushed.

***

Silence filled the warm air of the apartment, ripe with all of the unspoken words Philip couldn't seem to find the breath to say to his brother. Nigel sat across from him at the small table, his skin ashen and his eyes hollow. His hair fell limply across his forehead as he stared at the smooth surface of the wood.

There was much to be done—Philip knew they couldn't stay here after what had just happened—but still they sat. Too much had happened. God knows what would have happened had the *hermandades* succeeded in taking Nigel away. If they wanted to make a very painful point to him, they could have. If they wanted to kill him, they could have done so as well. Philip pressed his eyes closed. He couldn't bear it if something happened his brother.

"I thought you said you wouldn't come to my rescue again." Only a shadow of Nigel's former bravado darkened his voice. More than anything, Philip heard fear and dejection.

Meeting his eyes, Philip shook his head, suddenly tired. "I meant that I wouldn't rescue you from your own mistakes."

"And you didn't think that was my mistake?"

"Stealing from me was a mistake. Staying out all night was a mistake. Gambling again was a mistake. But taking the spoils that you won fairly?" Philip lifted a shoulder. "Those bastards were clearly out for blood."

Nigel shook his head, his brow gathered as though in thought. "I'm shocked you believed me."

Blowing out a long breath, Philip ran a hand through his hair. "The truth was in your eyes. Contrary to whatever you seem to think, I am not out to get you, Nigel."

He snorted. "Could have fooled me. I don't know why you had to drag me here anyway. Wasn't it enough to know that I was humiliated by the earl? Why were you so bloody determined to rub my face in it every chance you got?"

Tension draw tight Philip's already frayed nerves. "I didn't drag you here to rub your face in anything, Nigel. I brought you here to try to turn things around."

"No, you wanted to come here and play your little games and force me to see how worthless I really am."

"*What?*" Philip scrubbed his hands over his face, astounded at his brother's claim. "I came here *with you* in the futile hope that I could stop the runaway carriage wreck that I could see was about to happen. You're following the same path as our father, and I'm doing everything in my power to keep you from ending up just like him."

He glared back at Nigel, breathing hard from his outburst. Anger and helplessness and love for his brother battered him from the inside out. God, he'd almost lost him, and *still* his brother was fighting with him.

But Nigel merely watched him with shuttered eyes. "What do you care if I end up like Father? I'm sure you'd be glad to be rid of me."

Philip shook his head, at a complete loss as to how to respond to such an outrageous claim. "Did you *see* what I just did for you? Does that look like something I would do if I wished to be rid of you? Christ, Nigel, you're my only brother. I'd do anything to keep you from a fate like that. That's what I've been *trying* to do for weeks."

His brother's gaze dropped to the table again. His skin seemed even paler than when he'd come in, the bags beneath his eyes more pronounced. "Well, perhaps you should have just let them take me. I know you and Mother think I could have stopped the duel. I know you both blame me for him being dead now."

The words were like arrows piercing Philip's chest. God above, how could Nigel think such a thing? "That's ridiculous! We treated you like porcelain after Father's death. We made sure you could do no wrong."

Something flickered in his brother's dull eyes before he glanced down to his hands. "Nothing I did could get your attention in those days. I did more and more outrageous things, and nothing could turn your heads."

Philip stood there, blinking, trying to comprehend what his brother was saying. "You think we were turning our backs on you?"

"How could I not? I was practically invisible. The only thing that ever raised your ire was losing all that money to Malcolm. Not that I want it anymore. You can have the title, the wealth, the good standing, Mother's attention, and the adoration of debutantes everywhere. I've found my place among the gaming hells, brothels, and clubs of the *ton*."

Closing his eyes against the bitterness and hurt he heard in his brother's voice, Philip exhaled. "Nigel," he said when he could speak again. "I don't blame you for anything. I blame our father for ruining your innocence—I always have. We—Mother and I—didn't know how to make up for the pain he had put you through. We chose the path of never reprimanding or disciplining you, and obviously we chose wrong." He paused, waiting until Nigel's reluctant eyes met his. "You're my brother, and I love you. And whether you like it or not, I'm not going to give up on you."

The words echoed his conversation with Libby yesterday, but he pushed the thought away. The mere thought of her squeezed his battered heart, and he needed to focus on Nigel right now.

His brother's jaw worked as he pressed his eyes closed, clearly trying to gather himself. When he opened them, unshed tears shimmered, threatening to spill over. "Philip, you don't mean that. You—"

"I *do* mean it," he said, not letting his brother say another word. "All I've ever wanted is for you to be content in life. I want you to see that there is more to life than brothels and gaming hells and endless nights of nothingness. I want you to be the good, honorable man I *know* you can be."

Philip came to his feet, walked to his brother, and held out his hand. Cautiously, reluctantly, but with a glimmer of hope reflecting in his eyes, Nigel took his hand and allowed Philip to pull him up. There, as the breaking light of morning poured through the open windows and chased away the gloom of dawn, the two brothers embraced for the first time in years.

Sweet relief flowed through Philip's veins, and when they pulled apart, Nigel smiled at him in a way Philip hadn't seen him do since before their father's death.

"Does this mean that we can go home now? I'm not certain I want to be here if those men change there minds."

Nodding, Philip stepped back and gestured toward the room at large. "As soon as we can pack, we can go. I'm sure we can find passage on one of the outgoing ships if we hurry."

As his brother rushed to gather his things, Philip drew a long breath. More than anything, he wanted to go to Libby, to try to explain why he had deceived her. To apologize, to beg for forgiveness. But now wasn't the time. The look in her eyes had told him clearly enough that there was no way she would talk to him again anytime soon. He didn't want to leave things how they were, but right now, he had little choice.

It was time to leave Mr. Westbrook behind, and return to the Duke of Gillingham.

Chapter Nine

*L*ibby had thought leaving Spain behind would somehow also remove the almost-physical ache of her heartbreak. She now knew how naive she had really been. She'd been living with her aunt for over a month now, and she still found herself putting her hand to her heart, trying to soothe a pain that could never really be touched.

"Libby, dear, did you hear me?"

Blinking, she glanced over to her aunt, who watched her with empathetic gray eyes. "My apologies, Aunt Margaret. I'm afraid I was woolgathering." Her thoughts had once again turned to the man who didn't exist, wishing the dream of their time together had been real.

"That's perfectly all right, dear. I was hoping you could read the correspondence for me. Nothing brightens a rainy day quite like letters from friends."

Pasting a smile on her stiff lips, Libby nodded and reached for the pile of letters the butler must have brought in while Libby's mind had been in a courtyard in Spain.

Sorting through the letters, she said, "Let's see. We have one from Eleanor, one from Amelia—make that two, there's one for each of us—another from Lady Darley, and it looks like another for me." She frowned, not recognizing the handwriting on the thick packet. *What on Earth?*

"Let's start with Eleanor's," her aunt said, unaware of Libby's distraction. "I'm so looking forward to hearing more about the baby."

"Um, just a moment, if you don't mind. I-I have something in my eye." Dropping all the letters but one, she hurried from the room, not even sure why her heart had begun to pound. As soon as the door was shut behind her, she pulled open the packet.

The first page was mostly blank, with only one sentence written in thick, bold letters. Her hand flew to her mouth as she recognized the words as Spanish. She pored over them, easily translating them in her mind:

Every butterfly deserves a place to call home.

That was it. No signature, no other explanation. Shaking her head, she shuffled the papers, attempting to make sense of the other three pages. It was all very legal and official sounding. It was only when she saw a paragraph titled *Description* that she realized what she held.

A deed.

In her name.

Had he truly bought her a cottage by the sea? But his name was nowhere to be seen, not under any section. Only *Elizabeth Anne Abbington*, and an address: *13 Seashell Drive*.

She flipped to the last page, which contained only two sentences:

> *Though I don't deserve it, I hope that you may someday forgive me. If that day should be today, then you've only to step outside.*

Libby gasped, her hand flying to her heart. This time, instead of the ache she had grown so accustom to, hope sprang to life. *Could he really be here?*

Not pausing to think, to feel, or even to worry, Libby bolted for the front door. To the butler's great surprise, she wrenched it open and rushed outside, only to come up short, her heart thundering in her ears.

There, on the driveway before her, Philip stood completely alone, patiently waiting for her. The rain had slowed to a drizzle, but his fine clothes and uncovered hair were well soaked. So many emotions flickered across his face—relief, caution, hope, joy—all the things she herself was feeling as she stood at the top of the steps, looking down at him.

He smiled, a small, boyish grin that made her heart melt. *"Buenas tardes, bonita."*

She bit back an almost giddy grin. His pronunciation was horrible, but she knew what he meant. *Good afternoon, beautiful.* She hesitated for only a moment before offering a small smile in return. "Good afternoon." She didn't even try to choose a name to call him. *Philip* seemed much too intimate for a duke, but she didn't know if she would ever think of him as *Your*

Grace. Your Grace was a person she didn't know.

"You came," he said simply.

She nodded, suddenly shy.

He gazed up at her, his dark lashes spikey from rain. "My dearest Libby, I hope you can forgive me for deceiving you. It was never about you, but I should have told you the truth. The woman I was falling in love with deserved to know who I really was."

She sucked in a breath, her heart shuddering to a stop before surging back even faster than before. He had been falling in love with her? Her cautious hope from earlier bloomed brighter still.

"The thing is, you *did* know who I was," he said, stepping forward and slowly climbing the wide limestone steps. "More so than any other person in the world. The parts of me that I shared with you, I've never shared with anyone else." He reached the top step and paused, his gaze locking with hers. "I was wrong to deceive you, but what was between us was as honest as I've ever been."

She closed her eyes, breathing in the familiar scent of him as she savored his closeness. Looking to him once more, she said, "I forgive you, but I still don't know what that means. What about my uncle? Or your title? Or a hundred other little things that no longer seem to fit between us."

Smiling softly, he stepped forward until they were mere inches apart. "Oh, Libby," he breathed, sending a little chill chasing down her back. "We fit. We fit in every way that counts."

He slipped his hands beneath her jaw, cradling her face gently. He leaned down, setting off a riot of butterflies in her stomach as his lips came so close she could feel the heat of him against her mouth. "You're smart, strong, quick-witted, and beautiful," he said, his breath caressing her with each word. "You're kind, and brave, and adventurous. And best of all?" He paused, making her whole body burn with anticipation. "Best of all, our lips fit just so."

He kissed her then, pressing his mouth hard against hers, proving exactly how well they fit. It was the kind of kiss she had always dreamed of, stealing her breath and even making her toes curl right there by her aunt's open front door.

When at last he pulled away, he lowered his hands to hers, lacing them together tightly.

"I'm not going to let your uncle dictate my happiness, just as I hope you won't allow my station to dictate yours. As far as I'm concerned, you, my love, are perfect for me.

"Now, having said all of that, and with the promise that the cottage is yours no matter what . . . Elizabeth Anne Abbington, will you allow me to court you?"

"You wish to *court* me?" For some reason, she hadn't expected him to offer such a thing.

"No, I wish to marry you, but I realize that you may want some time to get know me, warts, titles, and all."

The thing was, standing here in his arms, she knew beyond a shadow of a doubt that she *did* know him. Even without knowing his name, she knew everything about him that mattered. She knew of his kindness, his willingness to stand by those he loved, his open-mindedness, and, despite it all, the upstanding nature of his character.

She thought of the past few years, how she had never really found the place where she felt she truly belonged. As he had so astutely pointed out, she'd simply had been flitting from one place to the next. But he'd changed all that because truly, that's what he felt like to her.

Home.

Wetting her lips, she met his warm gaze. "Perhaps you should ask me what you really wish to know."

He froze, his eyes wide. After a moment, he drew in a slow, deep breath and said, "My dearest Libby, will you marry me?"

Libby didn't even try to stop the tears that sprang to her eyes and slipped down her cheeks, cleansing away the heartache of the last month. She nodded, over and over again, smiling so broadly it hurt.

"Is that a yes?" he replied, grinning hugely, obviously knowing full well that it was.

"Yes," she exclaimed, the word as full of joy as she was. *"Si! Oui! Etiam! Ja, da, vai, evet—"*

She broke off when he lifted her from her feet and laughed with delight as he pressed his lips to hers in a deliciously sweet kiss. "I love you, Philip, no matter what your name or title may be."

Setting her back on her feet, he slipped his hands back in hers. "And I love you, Libby Abbington. And I will *really* love it when you will become Her Grace, The Duchess of Gillingham."

She scrunched up her nose, though she couldn't

have wiped away her smile to save her life. "I suppose I can live with *Duchess*, but *only* if you promise call me Mrs. Westbrook on our honeymoon.".

Epilogue

*L*eaning against the railing of the third floor balcony, Libby breathed in the warm, damp morning air and sighed happily. It had stormed during night, making the cozy atmosphere of their rented townhome that much more intimate. It had made for a rather delectable evening. She smiled, hugging her arms around her middle and holding tight the memory of Philip's capable hands exploring every inch of her to the music of the falling rain.

As if summoned from her thoughts, warm, strong arms wrapped around her from behind. Philip tugged her gently against the solid wall of his chest as his lightly stubbled jaw slid along the sensitive skin of her cheek. "*Buongiorno*," he murmured, his voice still rough from sleep.

She shivered with pleasure, burrowing deeper

into his arms. This was her absolute favorite part of the day. In the early morning hush, there was no *Your Grace* or *Duke* or *Duchess*; they were simply Philip and Libby, madly in love newlyweds. These were the moments when she could center herself, preparing for whatever the day may bring.

Philip had been wonderful about her role as duchess, making it clear that her only obligation was to love him, but she found she enjoyed being by his side and helping to run their households. Of course, she was also immensely grateful for his mother, who had welcomed her with open arms. Not only had she helped smooth the transition, but more importantly, she had provided the motherly love Libby had so desperately missed. It was easy to see where Philip's kindness had come from.

"Good morning," she replied, the words coming out on a blissful sigh.

"I'm surprised you're up this early, given your rather late night."

Even though it was just the two of them, alone above the empty piazza, the heat of a blush warmed her cheeks. "Mmm, the same could be said of you," she teased. "Nothing, however, could make me miss out on the glory of a Roman sunrise."

He tightened his hold and pressed a kiss to the side of her neck. "And nothing could make me miss out on the glory of seeing you bathed in the golden light of morning."

Reveling in the feel of his lips on her skin, she closed her eyes. "*Sei troppo dolce.*" *You're too sweet.* Not that she was complaining—quite the opposite, in fact.

He chuckled, and she could feel the rumble of his chest against her back. "I do so love when you speak Italian to me. Or Spanish, or Latin, or anything else you care to learn. It's *molto bello,*" he said, swinging the syllables in a surprisingly good impression of the way the locals spoke.

Smiling in utter contentment, she leaned back against him and watched as the first streaks of dawn fanned out over the city, lighting the magnificent buildings of both past and present. This morning they were in Rome, next week they'd be in Switzerland, and by next month they'll have made their way back to England, but no matter where they were, so long as she was wrapped in the arms of her husband, Libby was home.

Author's Note

As an author of Regency-set historical romance, I spend a lot of time in early 19th century England (and I love every minute!). With this book, however, I was excited by the possibility of heading somewhere a little more exotic. I had great fun researching all the wonderful places in Seville that Philip and Libby could have explored. In the end, I decided to take a bit of liberty with one of their visits: *Museo de Bellas Artes.* The museum was established in 1839, so while the building would have been there, I'm not certain the nuns who lived there would have allowed them in for a tour ;)

About the Author

Despite being an avid reader and closet writer her whole life, Erin Knightley decided to pursue a sensible career in science. It was only after earning her B.S. and working in the field for years that she realized doing the sensible thing wasn't any fun at all. Following her dreams, Erin left her practical side behind and now spends her days writing. Together with her tall, dark, and handsome husband and their three spoiled mutts, she is living her own Happily Ever After in North Carolina.

Find her at www.ErinKnightley.com, on Twitter.com/ErinKnightley, or at facebook.com/ErinKnightley

Printed in Great Britain
by Amazon